Montana Baby

Montana Baby

A Calhouns of Montana Romance

Juanita Kees

TULE
PUBLISHING

Montana Baby

Dedication

For my beautiful, faithful, furry friend, Sam, who kept me company throughout this book—until writing The End—before crossing the rainbow bridge. You're in my heart forever.

Acknowledgements

They say it takes a village to raise a child. The same could be said for a book-baby. Where would I be without my tribe?

Firstly, thank you to the team at Tule Publishing for taking on this series. The care and support I received during edits was truly heart-warming. The covers are stunning, thank you, cover fairies. What Tule achieves is amazing and I'm proud to be a part of it.

Secondly, a very big thank you and a huge hug for Ann B Harrison whose encouragement and support has been consistent throughout my writing journey. Thank you for believing I could bring the Calhouns and their garage to life.

PJ, thank you for the advice and pointing me in the right direction when I couldn't see the forest for the trees.

Kerrie and Lily, the two of you rock feedback and I love you both.

Lastly, to my critique group: Anna, Susy, Claire and Teena, thank you for loving the Calhouns. Lorraine, we miss you. Please come home.

Not forgetting my family who support me all the way. Without you, dinner would never reach the table and my tea would always be cold.

Dear Reader,

Thank you for visiting Calhoun Customs Garage. I hope you enjoyed Chase and Charlie's story. The most important thing in an author's journey to the next book is feedback from our readers, so please do leave a review. It would be valuable and appreciated.

I am a huge NASCAR and V8 Racing fan, so research for this story was so much fun. Any errors in the portrayal of the industry, racing rules and terminology are my own. The characters are completely fictional, although I wish a few of them were real!

If you'd like to keep up to date with what's next at Calhoun Customs Garage, please visit my website or sign up for my newsletter. I respect your privacy, and with that in mind, only issue about four newsletters per year.

Thank you for your company and I hope to see you back soon for book 2, Fast Lane.

Regards, Juanita

Chapter One

CHASE TOSSED THE doctor's report onto the scarred Formica table and turned to the view of Bigfork Bay—a sight that soothed his scattered thoughts and calmed the edginess growing in his belly. It hurt too much to think about his dad being diagnosed with Parkinson's. A disease that would steal his mobility, his independence and creativity, and the dream they'd built together at Calhoun Customs Garage.

As if life hadn't stolen enough from the Calhouns, Chase would have to bring home his siblings to more bad news. None of them had ever given thought to their father's mortality. Not Marty Calhoun, larger than life, tougher than nails, with a heart full of love for his children.

Chase lifted the carton of milk from the refrigerator and tested its weight. Mason had drunk all the damn milk again. And where was the sandwich Chase had left on the top shelf last night?

He walked out of the small kitchen into the garage. "Hey, Dad. Your coffee will have to be a while. Mason drank all the milk. I'll need to go over to Molly's to buy more."

Marty chuckled. His hand shook a little on the wrench

clenched in his palm. He rested his forearm on the fender of the '57 Chevy they were restoring for use on the ranch. "A growing boy needs calcium."

"He's twenty-nine. Shouldn't he be done growing by now?" Chase leaned on the opposite fender with a grin, ducking his head under the hood. "She's a beauty."

"She will be when she's done." His father sighed. "Not sure my hand will be steady enough to do the artwork Carter wants. Any response to that advertisement in the paper for a graphics artist?"

Chase pushed aside a stab of sadness. His dad would take the loss of his art hard. Harder than not being able to lift a wrench anymore. "No takers."

"Have you spoken to your sister about coming home at the end of the NASCAR season?"

"Not yet, Dad. I'm going to FaceTime her over coffee. Will you be okay here on your own? I won't be long, and Mason should be in as soon as he's helped Carter with the horses at the ranch."

Marty snorted. "I'm not darn useless yet, boy."

Chase grinned and gripped his father's shoulder, secure in knowing his dad would fight this disease with every ounce of his iron will. With the same spirit he'd fought for everything in his lifetime. "I'll be back soon."

He walked through into the showroom, his eye on the Montana sky outside the windows. The white-capped Swan Range Mountains soared above the river that snaked its way around the town, edged by the hectic colors of fall. Sunlight reflected off the bay where a group of boys fished off the dock.

Pushing through the side door, he crossed the road to Molly's Old Time Five and Dime. The thought of Molly made him smile. Everyone had told her it was time for a name change, that five and dime stores were a thing of the past. But Molly, fourth generation owner of the store she'd inherited from her father, had pretty much told them all to mind their own business. *It's always been a five and dime and that's what it'll stay.*

He opened the door and held it so Mrs. Thomas, bundled up in a warm coat and colorful scarf, could slip inside ahead of him. He closed it behind him, cutting off the icy blast of air blowing straight down the mountains.

A handful of customers wandered the aisles as he picked up a quart of milk from the double-door refrigerator and made his way to the checkout. Ahead of him, a young woman soothed a baby snug in a wrap-type carrier thing with straps over her shoulders and tied around her waist, kinda like a backpack for babies except in front.

"That'll be ten dollars, please, honey." Molly held out her hand and peered into the wrap. "How old is the baby?"

"She's three months old."

"They're adorable when they're so young. Every day there's something new they discover." Molly smiled warmly.

"So true." The young woman searched the carryall and pulled out her wallet to pay.

Her fingers hovered over a credit card before she selected

cash instead. Chase shifted his feet and looked over her shoulder to see what she'd bought. A packet of Molly's homemade chocolate chip cookies. A pint of milk and a newspaper. A bar of soap, a travel-sized pack of laundry detergent and a can of beans.

He looked at her. A long blonde braid snaked over her shoulder. He caught the scent of a pleasant perfume as she turned to look at him apologetically. About twenty-five, green eyes with a hint of attitude touched by tired. Her captivating eyes widened in surprise as they met his before her glance quickly shifted back to the goods on the counter and she moved a step or two away. Not the reaction he was used to from women, even ones with babies, which fascinated him even more.

The baby fussed, and the woman hushed it as she handed a twenty-dollar bill over to Molly.

Molly took the cash and rung it up. The cash register dinged as the drawer released and she selected the change. "You new in town, honey?"

Green Eyes rocked on the balls of her feet, eager to leave. What had he done to make her nervous? "Yeah, just arrived."

"Well, welcome to Bigfork. Where are you staying?"

"I … I have a reservation over at the Swan Inn." She stashed the change, dropped her wallet in the carryall and gathered the baby closer to her in the carrier. "I've got to go, sorry."

He could almost taste her sudden need to get away. Skittish. As if staying in one spot too long had consequences and

4

Molly's questions were making her nervous. A woman alone, new in town with a small baby, clearly a little on edge. Something about her didn't quite add up. Not when the Swan Inn was closed for renovations because of a recently burst water main. He was intrigued enough to delay her escape, his inner warning system on alert.

Chase narrowed his eyes and studied her profile. "It's cold out there. Maybe you should add one of Molly's famous hot chocolates to your order."

She looked at his boots instead of his face. "Maybe another time."

He rocked back on his heels, trying to keep it casual. "No time like now."

Her green gaze slammed into his, the message in them clear. *Back off.* Regardless of her warning, he couldn't deny the attraction that tugged at his senses. Pretty would be too tame a word to describe her alabaster skin and Nordic beauty. Stunning would be admitting his knees had lost the power to hold him up. And he had no hope of denying she stole his breath away, because it took him a couple of heartbeats to find his words.

"Cookies aren't enough for breakfast. Why don't you try one of Molly's famous breakfast muffins too? My treat."

Her chin went up, a stubborn lift that made him want to take it between his forefinger and thumb and study the lips she'd pulled into a firm line.

"Okay. Thank you." Her nonchalant shrug contradicted the urgent tap of her foot.

Molly dropped the items into a packet and added the muffin. "Here you go, honey. Caramel and banana. My favorite."

"Thank you." The woman hitched the carryall up over her shoulder with one hand and patted the baby with the other. She turned the full power of her gaze and a strained smile on Chase. "And thank you."

His gut tightened in harmony with another part of his anatomy which had no business reacting to a woman with a baby. Then she walked away, leaving him feeling like he'd been Tasered by Sheriff Hutchins, and with an itchy feeling in his gut.

"That was a very sweet thing to do, Chase Calhoun." A smile lifted Molly's lips, wrinkling her already wrinkled face further, her nod making the pompoms on her knitted beanie jiggle.

Heat crept up his neck to warm his cheeks. "Yeah. Well..." Something about her had him wanting to follow her out the door and ask more questions. Something that shouted fish-out-of-water.

Molly frowned as she added his quart of milk to the register and held out her hand for payment. "I thought George closed the inn?"

He counted the cash out onto her palm before answering, "Same. Maybe he kept a couple of the undamaged rooms open. I might give him a call to ask." If the place was damp, it might not be the best place for Green Eyes and her baby to stay. His gaze strayed to the window and the view beyond it.

"Hmmm." Molly dropped the coins into the cash register and closed the drawer.

He looked at her. "What does 'hmmm' mean exactly, Miss Molly?"

She looked back at him over the top of her purple-framed glasses and smiled. "I haven't seen you look at a girl like that in a long time."

"A man can look as long as he doesn't touch. Touching can get a man into an awful lot of trouble. Wrap it up, sweetheart, or Dad will be cranky by the time I get back." He leaned forward and kissed her cheek with affection.

Molly had been like a grandmother to the Calhoun tribe, keeping them all in line when they'd tested their father's patience. And with their mom gone, they'd needed her gentle, guiding touch. A lot.

She handed him his quart of milk. "You tell him I said hello. And maybe take that girl a thermos of tea. It'll be a while before the day warms up some." Molly nodded at where the young woman made her way over to the grassy area near the dock. "Oh, before I forget … I thought I saw a light on over at the garage last night, when I was locking up around eleven."

Chase frowned. Impossible. He'd checked all the lights were out and the doors locked before he'd left. And he'd activated the showroom and garage alarms. Perhaps Mason had come back to the shop after the races up at Binney Hill.

"Thanks, Molly. Where exactly?"

"Upstairs in the attic."

Okay, now that was strange. No one went into the attic anymore. All that was up there were a ton of obsolete parts his father refused to throw away and a lifetime of sad memories that made him afraid to climb the stairs.

He shrugged. Strange things had been happening ever since Mason had come home. He'd put it all down to his brother settling back in. "Maybe it was Mason looking for something up there. You work too hard, Molly, keeping such late hours."

Molly laughed. "What else is an old girl like me to do in this town?"

"Get some rest, go see a movie, come hang out with us at the ranch. We'd like that." He made a note to ask his brother about his late-night monkey business, along with what had happened to his missing chicken salad sandwich. The itch that had settled in his gut shifted to between his shoulder blades. Sometimes the memories that breathed in the attic still had the power to haunt them.

CHARLIE CUDDLED ZOE closer as she walked the short distance to the dock where the river ran into Bigfork Bay. The early morning chill bit into her cheeks. She pulled the protective covering of Zoe's carrier higher to cut out the wind and keep her warm. How much longer could they survive on borrowed chicken salad sandwiches and milk?

She'd not expected to find her father's PI, Ed Sullivan on her tail so quickly. Or the job waiting for her in Kalispell to be gone. The delay in getting there due to her car breaking down in Minneapolis had not been part of her big plan either. The reason Ed had found her was because she'd had no choice but to use her credit card to rent a replacement.

She'd planned every step of this trip to the nth degree, each stop, each room, each gallon of gas, each dollar of her expenses, right down to care for Zoe in the hours while she worked. Their breakaway, hers and Zoe's. The stand she'd had to take or remain under her father's control and allow him to make the decisions about Zoe's future. Adoption being at the top of that list.

Going back was not an option. Not while her father remained stubbornly inflexible. Not while she was determined to prove she had changed and could take care of her baby. For the sake of the most precious, life-changing gift ever.

So, despite the odds piling up against her, she'd kept moving. On to Bigfork. An unexpected stop on her agenda with a vacancy she could fill. Another dead end when she'd arrived to find the inn closed due to the damage from a burst pipe and the vacancy of receptionist no longer on the cards. Accommodation and a job washed away in whirlpool of water.

She cursed the choices that had driven Charlotte Jackson, NASCAR brat, out of Daytona Beach and into the wilds of Montana. All she'd wanted was to establish her independence before she had to face her father again. Instead the fates had turned the tables and she'd had no choice but to resort to desperate measures.

"He won't succeed, Zoe. He won't make us come home. I won't let him take you away."

She had to make this work, find a way around the curve ball fate had thrown her. Curve balls. She hadn't expected to face another one in the man behind her at the checkout. Heat flushed through her. Kind, warm eyes that reminded her of blue summer skies, and a voice like smooth, top-shelf brandy. And then he'd treated her to a muffin, as if she hadn't taken enough from him already.

But desperate times called for desperate measures and using her credit card again would only bring Ed Sullivan roaring into town, hot on the trail of her transactions. She shivered at the thought. As much as she hated what she'd had to do, it had seemed like the safest place to hide while she kept her dwindling cash supply in her pocket and her whereabouts a secret for as long as she could.

She'd felt the inexplicable pull of the attic above the Calhoun's garage the moment she'd seen the reflection of the setting sun on the window. As if someone had whispered her name and taken her by the hand. She'd been drawn to the staircase at the back of the building that led up to a door. The door had been bolted shut with a lock on it, but she'd found a loose panel she could wiggle through.

She'd debated long and hard on the consequences, when her only other option would have been to sleep in the car. But that would be too cold for Zoe and it would certainly attract the attention of the local sheriff. So, she'd grasped the idea and found a warm, safe, secure place to sleep. And when it came time, she'd explain to the Calhouns why she'd made the choice she had.

She settled Zoe in for a feed, covering her with a baby blanket, and nibbled on the muffin, alternating with sips of milk as she absorbed the peace of her surroundings. The rustle of the wind in the trees, the lap of the water against the shore. Laughter off the street, whoops from the boys fishing on the dock. No shouting or arguing. No one forcing her to make decisions she didn't want to make about adoption. Pushing the blanket back a little, she traced a finger down Zoe's cheek, her heart full of love. How had she created a human being so beautiful? She couldn't undo the poor choices that had brought Zoe into the world, but she could do everything in her power to secure her baby's future and be a good mom.

Heavy footfalls rustled the fallen leaves on the grass. "We meet again."

She looked up at the sound of Chase Calhoun's voice. "We do."

No longer hedged in by questions and small spaces, the unease his earlier presence had raised, eased a little. A twinge of regret pinched at her belly. She hated telling lies, even small ones that would protect her and her baby.

Long legs encased in denim, a black long-sleeved T-shirt emblazoned with the Calhoun Customs logo under a thick jacket, opened by one hand pushed into the pocket of his jeans. Holy hotness. Another time, another place, and she might have been interested. A time before she'd become solely responsible for another precious life. Still, Chase Calhoun was eye candy, and there was no harm in appreciating his presence.

"I'm Chase Calhoun."

"I know."

He frowned. "I guess you're one up on me then," he said as he held out a thermos.

"I'm Charlie."

"Hi, Charlie. We kinda got off on the wrong foot earlier. I brought you some herbal tea to go with that muffin as a peace offering. Molly said coffee wouldn't be good for you when you're … you know …" He waved a hand at where Zoe had let go of her breast, exposing her naked skin to the cold.

She tugged the blanket up to cover Zoe as she reattached. "Thank you again."

Chase leaned down to place the thermos on the grass next to her. "You're welcome. So, I'm guessing if you've only just arrived in town, you're killing time until check-in? Do you like cars?"

The irony of his questions had her lips curving against her will. If only he knew. "I like custom-built cars. I'm a fan of your dad's work. He's a genius in design and graphics." The moment she'd seen the sign above the garage, she'd recognized she was in Calhoun country and her sketching fingers had started to itch.

He laughed. "Dad would love hearing that. How about I give you a tour of the garage when you return the thermos later? It will get you out of the wind for a while."

Excitement trickled through her bloodstream. "I'd like that, thank you." No way would she pass up the opportunity to appreciate the beauty and craftsmanship of a Calhoun custom build up close rather than in magazines.

His mouth curved in a smile that almost stopped her heart. A smile filled with pride and excitement that spoke of his passion for the garage. The kind of passion she wanted to harness and capture, to release back into the artwork that came alive on their custom builds.

"I guess I'll see you later then." He took a few steps backward, retreating slowly.

"Later."

She watched him walk away for the pure beauty of it. One hand in the pocket of his short-length jacket, the other raking through his hair, hips that moved with grace and an invitation that brought a different kind of rhythm to mind. An ass that begged for a starring role in a Levi's commercial. Long legs that made short work of the distance as they carried him out of reach.

On the dock, the boys packed up their rods and their catch, ready to move on. Waves lapped at their feet as the wind that swirled through the bay whipped up a swell. She shivered and reached for the thermos, careful to keep it away from Zoe. Securing it between her knees, she unscrewed the top and poured the liquid into the plastic cup. Not too hot, not too cold. Perfect.

In her spot, sheltered by the trees, Charlie sipped the tea, enjoying the view and flipping through the newspaper until Zoe finished feeding. Her attention snagged on an ad for a graphics artist and her heart pounded against her ribs. Maybe the fates were smiling on her after all. In the most unexpected way. A design artist at Calhoun Customs was her dream come true. And she'd embrace the opportunity she'd been given with both hands.

Warm, content, energized, she cleared her impromptu picnic, threw the wrappers and carton in the nearby trash can, then dropped the thermos into her carryall. She tucked the blanket around Zoe's wrap carrier to ward off the chill of the walk ahead and tried to suppress the excitement of seeing Chase again in the comfort of his own environment. Chase Calhoun was a nice guy and, if she was successful in gaining an interview, her prospective employer. That was all he could be to her.

Expectation fired her imagination as she walked the short distance up the main street to Calhoun Customs Garage. She peered in through the big windows. Up front, examples of their work took pride of place. A Studebaker restored to its original state—polished chrome and baby-blue paint, whitewall tires and cereal bowl hubcaps. A '66 Mustang in cherry red with black stripes and a mean air scoop on the hood, flares on the rear, and chrome wheels no one would dare let loose on a racetrack for fear of damage. A Pontiac Trans Am with artwork all over it that made her heart thump with excitement. This was where she wanted to be. With people who had a passion for the car not the race, for the power and beauty not the win.

She looked left toward a shadowy corner in the back where a project stood hidden under cover with no hint of what might be underneath. To the right, a low wall ran the length of the showroom, topped by windows that showcased the garage where the restorations took place.

Behind the glass, Chase leaned on the fender of a '57 Chevy, deep in conversation with Marty Calhoun, track legend and the artist she'd always dreamed of meeting. The Calhouns had a vision her father would never have. Custom design, an art her father considered a hobby not a career, but something the Calhouns took seriously.

Charlie opened the door and entered the showroom. The faint scent of polish and leather teased her senses. She moved to the Trans Am and ran her hand over the smooth surface of the artwork. Not a decal anywhere. Only art, airbrushed directly on the body with a steady hand, the way she wanted to do it. She sensed Chase rather than saw him as his shadow crossed the hood under the spotlights. He filled the space beside her.

"How was the tea?"

She smiled. "Perfect, thank you. Is this your dad's work?"

Pride lit his features before it was chased by sadness. "Yeah. He struggles to keep a steady hand these days. He's in the early stages of Parkinson's disease. We've had to advertise for an artist to take over the work."

"That's so sad." She couldn't imagine a world without his designs. It would be the end of an era in custom cars.

"He wants to find someone he can mentor in the way we do things to prepare for a time when he can't do it anymore. Dad's a tough guy. He'll keep doing it until he finds the right person to take over." He nodded toward the garage. "Come on in and meet him. He's expecting you."

Chase stepped back for her to precede him, guiding her with a light hand on her elbow. She liked the gentleness of his touch, the comfort and reassurance in it, the pleasant tingle of goose bumps it created on her skin. She stepped into the garage with its sealed floors and walls lined with tool drawers and equipment. Excitement rippled through her again. Back home, she'd been allocated to a desk, designing team merchandise or collating images for advertising and articles in their team magazine.

This was the real thing. This was the hands-on stuff she'd dreamed of doing. She stepped toward the Chevy and her fingers itched for sketch pad and pencils to create a design for the hood and the sides. Maybe even one for the tailgate.

Marty Calhoun straightened as she approached. "You must be Charlie."

She held out her hand. "It's an honor to meet you, Mr. Calhoun."

"Call me Marty." He shook her hand with only the slightest tremble to his fingers. "So, what do you think about the place?"

"It's everything I expected it to be and more."

"Well, that's a good thing, right? And who is this?" He nodded toward the bundle under the blanket.

"This is Zoe, my little girl." Pride touched her voice as she peeled back the blanket. Zoe slept peacefully snuggled inside the carrier.

"Been a long time since my kids were that small." Marty smiled. "What brings you to Bigfork in the fall? Most folks prefer to hang out here in the summertime when the water's warmer and the fish are biting."

"I had a job lined up in Kalispell, but it fell through. So, I kept going and found Bigfork."

And if the Calhouns were looking for a graphic design artist, this could be her and Zoe's new hometown, their new life. Her lucky break. The perfect job, except it would be in the enemy's camp. That wouldn't go down well with her father. Could she afford the risk? Not let an old feud stop her from grasping this opportunity when she needed it so badly? Yes, she could. Wasn't that what finding her independence was all about? Standing up for what she believed in rather than allowing her father to make her decisions for her?

"You're not from around here, are you? Do I detect an East Coast inflection?" Marty's question stilled her thoughts.

Charlie wrinkled her nose. "Florida, mostly, but my family traveled a lot."

"Brave move coming all the way over from Florida with a baby to start a new job."

Her father would call it rebellious. Her mother would say

it was stupid and irresponsible. She'd prove them wrong. "It's time I made a life for Zoe and me outside the family circle."

"Hmm…" Marty studied her carefully. "You look kinda familiar. Do I know your family?"

Her breath hitched in her throat. With her black and pink hair dye and heavy makeup long gone, she looked a lot like her mom, who was easily recognizable through her charity work and society page appearances. If the Calhouns knew who she was, would they still be prepared to consider her for the artist's job? Would they give a job to the daughter of a man who hated them and everything their success stood for? Doubt edged into her thoughts, making her take a step back as she tried to think of an answer.

Chase stepped in with a touch to her shoulder. "Dad knows so many people, he sees someone he recognizes in everyone." He offered her a smile that did little to settle the thoughts chasing each other through her mind. "The Chevy Dad's working on belongs to my brother, Carter. He has a few running around the ranch he wants restored and painted. Why don't I show you the rest of the setup? We recently installed a spray booth with a high-tech extraction system to minimize fumes during spraying and airbrushing."

She followed Chase to the rear of the garage where the booth stood empty and silent, the double doors closed and the lights off. Could she do this? The airbrushing she'd done had been in less sophisticated places than this. Backyard painting projects done in secret, in the company of people her parents would turn their noses up at. Artwork they snubbed as little more than somewhat stylish graffiti.

"It's fully automated, so it's a case of simply selecting the program you want. Makes things a lot easier when we're doing undercoats and topcoats on whole bodies. Shaves off a lot of the waiting time."

Chase's words eased the doubt. She could learn to work with new technology. For Zoe. For herself. She had to take one last rebellious stand. There'd be too much to lose if she didn't. "I saw your advertisement in the paper for a graphics artist. Airbrush art is something I've always loved to do, but it's been more of a hobby than a career because there was no scope for it in the job I did back in Florida."

Interest fired in his eyes. "Have you worked on custom designs before? You said you were a fan."

"I did airbrushing privately, but it was backyard art for a small clientele. I'd be happy to show you some of my work?" Her heart beat a nervous tattoo in her chest.

"I'd like to see it and I'm sure Dad would too. How about you drop by with it tomorrow? I'd say we do it this afternoon, but we've got a big reveal scheduled for today."

His smile widened with encouragement and fresh hope bloomed in her chest. For once, the skills she'd learned as a rebellious teenager could be used to get her out of trouble instead of into it. "I'd like that. Tomorrow morning it is."

"It's a date." He held out his hand to shake on it, his fingers closing around hers as she placed her palm against his.

She ignored the lurch of excitement in her belly that

came from more than the promise of an official interview. "Thank you for giving me a chance."

"You're welcome. So, have you checked in at the Swan Inn yet?"

Charlie stiffened. How to answer that one? She'd prefer him not to know quite yet that she'd arrived in town last night and had to take refuge in the attic above his garage. "Er … no, not yet." Evading the question wasn't lying, right? Guilt niggled at her again. She hated having to do what she'd done, but she'd had little choice.

"Well, then you probably don't know that the inn is inhabitable due to a burst water main."

Oh, she knew all right. That was what had put her in this pickle and thrown a huge sledgehammer on her well-laid-out plans. She'd make it up to them. She had to. "Oh."

"There is another inn about ten miles out of town."

"Thank you, I'll look it up."

"And make sure George gives you a refund if you've paid the deposit on the room."

"Okay, thank you. I'll see you tomorrow with my portfolio." Tomorrow, she'd confess to seeking refuge in their attic, explain the circumstances that had put her there. With a job secured, she could afford to pay out cash for a room somewhere and stay card-untraceable until she had her feet back under her. Tomorrow her future would begin.

Chapter Two

OUTSIDE CHASE'S CABIN an owl hooted, and laughter drifted up through the night from the ranch campsite where his younger brother, Carter, would be entertaining guests with stories around the bonfire, a perk they could all enjoy after a day in the garage.

Carter ... the brother the car gene had skipped. Instead he'd inherited their maternal grandfather's love of the land and had turned the family property into a lucrative tourist attraction that gave visitors the full ranch experience.

As much as Chase enjoyed coming home to the ranch at night, it was the garage that kept him buzzing. And today, he'd been buzzing with an excitement of a different kind. A dangerous kind when he couldn't afford to think with his heart instead of his head.

Charlie, a mystery that intrigued him. He'd waved her goodbye with a niggle in his gut. Something didn't add up. He couldn't deny he was attracted to her. What sane, fully functional, testosterone-driven male wouldn't be? She was a beautiful girl. One who possessed a certain kind of charm. The kind that wrapped a guy around her little finger and drew him in. A dangerous charm when his trustworthy instinct told him she wasn't being completely upfront with him.

He'd kept a close eye on her as she'd approached her rental car parked near Molly's store. He'd heard the chirp of the alarm before she'd opened the back door and unwrapped the carrier from around her, strapped the baby into a safety seat and closed the door. She'd made her way to the driver's door, checking up and down the street. Once. Twice. Three times. Looking for something. Or someone. He'd watched as she got in, started the car and pulled away from the curb. In the opposite direction of the inn he'd told her about.

She'd lied. He knew that, and while his bullshit detector never failed him, his gut told him there was a reason she'd lied. She'd asked questions but answered few. Evasive, carefully thought-out answers that had him wishing he had her resume, so he could read it tonight. Tomorrow, he'd interview her for the job and wait for her to come clean with him. The thought reminded him that he hadn't checked his emails to see if there'd been any other applicants for his advertisement.

Damn it. In all the excitement of Bobby Stuart's new car reveal, he'd left his laptop at the garage. Chase checked his watch. He could leave it till the morning, but with Charlie coming in tomorrow for an interview, he wanted to be sure of any other possibilities before he offered her the position.

And with her name on his mind and the questions it raised, came the thought of a pair of beautiful green eyes, and the picture of a woman nursing her baby, looking as if she held the most precious bundle in the world. A man shouldn't find that incredibly beautiful when there was most likely a baby-daddy in the mix somewhere.

Was that who she was running from? Now there was a situation he should be wary of, but something in her green eyes had called to him at a level that went beyond mere interest and his instinct told him there was more to her story.

He tossed his pickup keys in his hand. Thirty minutes from the ranch into town. If he hurried, he'd be back in time to share a last-call beer with Carter and his guests around the campfire. Carter, the only cowboy in their family. Unless he counted Mason, who gave "cowboy" a whole new meaning through speed and dare-devil stunts.

Chase pulled the door of his cabin closed and waved to Carter, standing on the porch of the main ranch house, as he crossed the distance to his truck.

"Going out?" Carter checked his watch. "Hot date?"

Chase grinned. "I wish. I left my laptop at the garage and I've still got work to do."

"I prefer my idea." His brother lifted a six-pack of local brew. "Will you be back in time for a beer?"

"Yeah. Make sure Dad goes easy, okay? His shakes were quite bad today."

"Yes, Mother."

"Smart-ass. Save me one." Chase slipped in behind the wheel of his pickup and gunned the motor. The V8 Chevy Silverado Redline roared to life, releasing a matching purr of satisfaction from Chase's lips. He loved nothing more than the sound of a V8 tuned to perfection by his brother. He might be more of a numbers man, but the Calhoun clan all ran on high-performance fuel instead of blood.

He took the drive easy, turning up the heat as the chill of the night snuck in through the cabin of his pickup. The lights of Bigfork twinkled below the night sky against the backdrop of the mountain range cloaked in shadows. He counted himself lucky to be born and raised in one of the best towns in the Flathead Lake district, a place he'd never contemplated leaving.

Pulling up at the garage, a sense of unease tickled his senses. He looked up at the attic, dark and full of buried memories. The reflection of the moon filled the window, covered by the curtains his mother had made. He shivered. How was it that dark, forgotten space still had the power to chill his bones and make his heart ache? He got out the truck and waved to Molly across the street, having a cigarette break outside her grocery store.

"Hey, Molly," Chase called.

"Back so soon, Chase?" She waved.

"Yeah, forgot my laptop."

"Oh?" Molly frowned. "I coulda sworn I saw a light in the attic again. Thought one of you boys might still be in the garage." She checked her watch. "Must have been the reflection of the moon. Better get back to it. Got shelves to restock before I head home."

"Have a good night, Molly. Take care now."

She blew him a kiss goodbye and Chase caught it against

his heart in the ritual they'd kept from his childhood. Then he made his way around to the side door, unlocked it, and pushed it open. Darkness cloaked the inside of the building, the only light coming from a dim glow of streetlights through the windows. He stilled the beep on the panel with a code to turn off the alarms that protected the garage and showroom and made his way to his office. Chase flicked on the light. Not there. Damn it, where had he left it? The kitchen.

He moved through to the back of the garage and turned on the light. His gaze fell on a can, all rinsed out and ready for recycling, on the counter. Well, at least Mason hadn't left it still full of sauce to attract bugs, but he had to talk to his brother about his late-night food fests at the garage. The last time Mason had all but moved back into the attic, he'd been a miserable, tortured soul, teetering on the edge of self-destruction. Chase didn't want to see that happen again.

But the attic gave Mason comfort where it had the opposite effect on Chase. The reason he hadn't installed an alarm in the old living areas at the back of the garage. So, Mason could come and go when he needed his space. There was nothing for thieves to steal back there except dusty old parts and confronting memories.

He checked the washroom off to the side. Yep, damp towels on the rail and the scent of soap still clinging to the air. A sensory memory niggled at the back of his mind. It fled at the sight of a pair of lacy panties on the floor. Aha! That explained it all. Mason must have a new love interest.

Good. It might stop him pining over Paige.

The thought of Paige reminded Chase he'd forgotten to call Trinity. He scooped up the panties with the waistband between his thumb and forefinger and tossed them in the direction of the plastic laundry basket. Which wasn't there. An uneasy feeling twisted his gut. It wasn't as if Mason would have thought to take the laundry home to do.

A mewling sound from the back recess of the garage reached his ears. So quiet he almost thought he'd imagined it. A stray cat? The noise came again, a little louder this time. He followed the sound to the attic stairs. A snuffled cry and a noise nothing like a cat's drifted down them. Dread gripped his gut along with an unhealthy sense of *deja vu* that stole his breath. Was he so tired that he was hearing noises, ghosts of the past?

He pushed away the memories of his mother's face, contorted in pain as she'd tried to stand, one hand gripping the metal railing on the stairs up to the attic, the other cupping her abdomen. *Chase.* Her desperate cry whispered through his mind.

With a frown, Chase shook off the memory, pressed down on the panic creeping through his blood, and took the metal steps one at a time, careful not to make a noise. There had to be a perfectly good explanation for all this. It had to be a cat seeking refuge from the cold.

At the top, he passed a row of abandoned car parts and walked straight into a clothesline covered with baby clothes and other delicate items. A bra, some panties and a familiar hoodie. He pushed his way under the line into a glow of light that didn't come from the moon in the window. A flashlight burned softly next to a makeshift bed, less than ten feet away.

There, in his washing basket, wrapped in a blanket, was Zoe, tiny fists waving in the air, snuffled mewling noises coming from pouty lips. And on the back seat of his dad's old Dodge Charger, lay Charlie fast asleep under a picnic blanket, a sketch pad open on the floor beside her.

Chase leaned his shoulder against the edge of a steel shelving unit. How had she ended up in their attic? And why had she lied? The thoughts that had plagued him earlier returned. The girl had something to hide and he'd find out what it was.

Long eyelashes brushed her cheeks in sleep. Lips made for kissing parted on the soft rhythm of her breathing. She most definitely didn't look like a criminal on the run. Just a tired young mother. An extraordinarily beautiful Sleeping Beauty like the one in the fairy tales his mom used to read to Grace. If he were that prince, he'd happily kiss her awake.

The baby let out a wail that killed any remotely romantic ideas forming in his mind. Green eyes fluttered open, muddled with sleep. She pushed herself up on her elbow and paused as if orientating herself to her surroundings before reaching for the bundle in the basket.

"Hey, baby. Is it feeding time already? Hush now." She cuddled the baby to her, making cooing noises that made Chase wish he was the one she held in her arms.

He waited in the shadows until the baby had settled and the hum of infant noises and soothing lullabies filled the air. It reminded him of a long time ago when his mom's soft singing had flowed through the attic space at night. There was something exceptionally beautiful about the bond between mother and baby, a sight he was more than happy to enjoy now that he knew he wasn't imagining things.

He let his words drift quietly into the almost-silence. "So that's what happened to my chicken salad sandwich."

TERROR RIPPED THROUGH Charlie, stealing her breath. Hunching over Zoe, hugging her tighter, she swept up a screwdriver into her fist and scrambled to her knees. At her breast, the baby protested the movement with a whimper.

"Hey, it's okay, Charlie. Relax, it's Chase. I'm not going to hurt you, honey." He stepped into the pool of light. "I'm sorry. I didn't mean to frighten you."

"Chase." She breathed, recognition filtering through her shock. Panic slowly faded from the thump against her rib cage as she soothed Zoe's full-blown cries. "It's okay," she whispered, willing her heart rate and her baby to settle.

"We meet again." He folded his arms across his chest. Booted feet planted apart, he stood in front of her makeshift bed, a solid six-foot-something wall of muscle.

Remnants of fear kept her tongue tied around the explanation milling in her mind. She searched his face in the soft light as he moved closer. The shadow of stubble on his jaw, his hair all mussed and the dimples in his cheeks drawn by a grim face rather than a smile.

"I can explain."

"You ate my beans." His corded arms unfolded, and he planted his big hands on his hips. "And my chicken salad sandwich."

"I replaced the beans with the can I bought today. And I'll make you another sandwich." Charlie cuddled Zoe closer as her cries settled.

"It's a deal." He nodded and looked around. "I like what you've done to the place." His gaze lasered in on hers, piercing blue. "But you can't stay here."

"Please let me stay. Just for tonight. I'll pay you the same rate as I would have paid at the inn. I wasn't expecting to be out of a job with no income, so I need to be careful with spending on my cash and cards. I'd planned to explain it all to you tomorrow." Her chest tightened as the words tumbled from her tongue.

Chase crouched in front her, the denim pulling tight over his thighs. She allowed herself to be distracted by the pale, worn material that clung lovingly to every curve and swell. The knot in her throat tightened.

He reached out to stroke Zoe's downy head, his fingers gentle as they brushed against the skin of Charlie's shoulder. "An attic full of old parts and dust and bugs isn't the place for a baby, Charlie."

"I have nowhere else to go." Desperation lent a plea to

her tone. "This was meant to be a new start for us. But things didn't quite go as planned."

Darn it, she hadn't meant to let so much slip, but Chase wasn't the kind of guy she could lie to. The tears she'd tried to hold back since losing the job in Kalispell, threatened to spill over. She brushed them away. For Zoe's sake, she had to stay strong.

He sighed and sat down on the old back seat next to her, stretching out his long legs. His warmth filled the space, the lingering spice of his cologne clinging to his skin. All male. And as sexy as hell. Exactly what she'd vowed to avoid since the night she'd been stupid enough to indulge in a rebellious one-night stand and bring shame to the Jacksons of Daytona Beach.

"Okay..." The deep baritone of his voice vibrated through her, skittered along her nerve ends and found the perfect place to lodge the pleasure the sound generated. He dragged a hand through his hair. "What about this offer, then ... I own a cabin on my brother's guest ranch. You can use my guest room until you sort things out."

"You'd do that for a stranger?"

He wrinkled a beautifully straight, strong nose with just a small bump in it. "Renting rooms to strangers is my brother's bread and butter. I think we can make a plan for you and Zoe. It'll be no different from renting a room at the inn."

"Only if you'll let me pay my way."

He held out a hand to shake hers. "Deal."

Charlie shook, his fingers strong and firm around hers, her palm encompassed by his. "If you're sure?"

He smiled, the dimples in his cheeks deepening. "If I leave you here and Molly finds out I haven't offered you some Calhoun hospitality, I'll be in big trouble. It's a lot better than having old muffler pipes and engine parts as company. I'd be happier knowing you're both safe and warm."

Chase pushed up off the seat in one fluid motion that flexed muscle and stretched denim in a way that made her wish she hadn't made so many bad choices in life. In another time and place, he would have made it onto her wish list, but that was a life-change ago. Her must-haves weren't the only priority anymore.

"Thank you." She breathed, heat rising on her neck, relief flooding her.

"How about I go over to Molly's and stock up on things you might need while you pack?"

Zoe squirmed and made noises, her little face a frown of concentration. "A pack of diapers might be a good idea. We go through a few of those."

He laughed, a sound that warmed her a little more. "When my sister, Trinity, was a baby, Dad didn't have time to wash cloth diapers and used disposables. We had them stacked high in all different sizes in the storeroom at the ranch. Being a single parent and raising six kids close together in age kept him busy."

She'd heard speculation about the reasons for Marty

Calhoun's departure from racing, but she'd never paid much attention to gossip. "That would have been hard."

He shook his head. "Not easy, but he did it." He turned away, but not before she caught the haunted look in his eyes. Chase Calhoun had challenges of his own. "I'll go and do some shopping before Molly closes the store. Where did you park your rental car? If you give me the key, I'll swap the baby seat over into mine. It will be easier to travel together than to give you directions out to the ranch in the dark."

Charlie hesitated. Leaving her car behind would be a gamble. She'd have no transport, no escape, if this new arrangement didn't work out. The Calhouns had a trustworthy reputation. Almost a celebrity status. They wouldn't do anything to harm her or Zoe. She'd be safe. And if the rental car stayed hidden, Ed wouldn't see it if he drove into town on her tail.

She reached for the carryall and retrieved the key. Holding it out to him, she said, "It's behind the old shed under the tree." He took the key, his fingers brushing hers and sending little tingles through her nerve endings, then he turned to walk away. "And Chase?"

He stopped at the makeshift clothesline. "Yeah?"

"Thanks. I swear I'll make it up to you."

His bright blue eyes roamed over her, assessing her and the bundle in her arms. Her heart did a little flutter against her ribs as she imagined them looking at her in a whole different way. Thoughts she shouldn't be having when that was exactly what had gotten her into this trouble in the first place.

"No running away while I'm gone, Charlie, okay?"

She shook her head. The time for running was over. She needed stability. For herself. For her baby. And maybe Bigfork would be the place she found it.

Chapter Three

CHASE PULLED THE collar of his jacket up around his ears. He walked across the street and pushed in through the glass door.

"Hi, Molly," he called as he passed by the counter, sweeping up a basket as he went.

He made his way down the aisles, stopping, checking and dropping baby stuff into his basket. The last thing he'd expected to be buying from Molly's Old Time Five and Dime on a Friday night was diapers. And the instant baby milk, which had been a tough choice given the range. And bottles, a sterilizing kit and a pacifier, just in case, because … well, hell, what did he know about breastfeeding when Trinity had been bottle-fed? He added a selection of herbal tea and chocolate to the basket.

Molly's eyebrows rose almost right into her hairline as Chase unpacked his purchases onto the counter. A slow smile spread on her lips as she eyed him over her glasses. "Someone in the Calhoun clan bring home a baby?"

"Something like that. Do I need this, Molly?" He tapped the plastic lid on the can.

"Maybe not if she's breastfeeding, but I know a lot of

moms who top up with formula at night. Some say it helps the baby sleep better. Fuller tummy, you know. If the baby sleeps better, her mom will sleep better too."

Mrs. Thomas emerged from the shelves behind him, her gasp of surprise at his basket of supplies carefully concealed behind her hand. Darn it, word would spread through the streets of Bigfork by morning, and by lunchtime he'd be pegged as the father of a mystery baby.

"I won't tell a soul that the big bad mamma bear of the Calhoun boys is really a soft touch." Molly winked. "And neither will you, Joan." She warned Mrs. Thomas.

Chase frowned. Molly was the second one tonight to refer to him as mothering. He sighed and opened his wallet. Being ten and in charge of your siblings was not something he'd thought he'd be doing the day he'd found his mom in a crumpled mess at the bottom of the attic stairs.

He pushed away the vision in his mind. It hurt to think about her. Mitch had been barely two years old at the time. Then their dad had come back a few days later with the baby and the bad news. Mom was never coming home.

He shook off the gloom and handed over his credit card. "Will I need anything else, Molly?"

She eyed his purchases as she processed the transaction. "I think you've got it covered, son. I'm guessing this is for our young lady from this morning? She wasn't staying at any of the inns around here, was she? Where did you find her?"

Chase grimaced. "In the attic."

"The attic? Oh dear, Chase, that would have given you a

bit of a shock. I'll admit that when I saw those lights going on and off, I wondered if your mom was trying to send me a message from the spirit world. Gave this old heart of mine a kick start, mind you. You'll help the girl out?"

He nodded. "How can I not, Molly? You'd never forgive me if I didn't."

He didn't want to explore his own reasons for it either. Certainly not the ones that raised the memories of another baby born and a life lost in that same place all those years ago. Yet he couldn't deny the draw of her green eyes, the white-blonde hair secured in a ponytail he wanted to loosen, and the glimpse of a body he wouldn't mind holding against him. And that was a feeling he hadn't had in a very long time. But he had to tread carefully since he had no desire to walk blindly into another man's territory. And where *was* the baby's father? What had brought Charlie to be alone with a baby in a strange town?

"You're a good boy, Chase Calhoun." Molly reached over and pinched his cheek hard. "Go now. Get that girl and the baby somewhere nice and warm."

Chase scooped up the grocery bags. "See you in the morning, Molly. Take care going home now. The roads are getting slippery at night. You too, Mrs. Thomas."

"You know I'm always careful." Molly waved him out the door.

Chase tossed the grocery bags into the back of the pickup, pleased now he'd chosen the dual cab version or he would've had to find another ride tonight. He went to locate

Charlie, half-expecting her to have had second thoughts and disappeared. He was a stranger offering her refuge miles out of town. And the way his thoughts ran when he saw her, she should be wary, because he couldn't honestly put her in the guest basket when his body and mind had her labeled as something more.

He found her in the kitchen, cleaning the table with disinfectant, Zoe gurgling away happily in her makeshift bed in the washing basket. For the first time Chase got to see the baby's face in full, having only had profile views before. Yeah, no doubts at all as to whom her mom was. Charlie might be guilty of something, but baby-napping could be crossed off the list.

"Hey, Zoe." He captured the little fist waving about and felt the baby-soft skin against his calloused fingers. She looked up at him, wide-eyed. "You ready for a ride out to the ranch? I've strapped your seat in and we're ready to roll." He looked at Charlie. "Ready to go?"

She nodded. "I guess."

"Right. Let's hit the road then." Doubt edged into his mind.

Was he doing the right thing? Should he have talked Mrs. Thomas into taking her in instead? No, that would drop her right in a pool of gossip at the next quilting club meet.

"Chase?" Charlie's hand settled on his arm, sending little shock waves roaring through his bloodstream. "Thank you."

He rubbed a hand across the back of his neck to stop

himself from covering her fingers with his. Damn it, he'd have to be careful around Charlie or he could find himself in a lot of trouble. Eager to keep his hands busy and away from temptation, he moved to pick up his laptop and her suitcase. "Let's get you and Zoe home."

Home. That sounded too comfortable. Too personal. He cursed inwardly. This girl had his tongue tied in knots in a way he didn't remember it being twisted before. Chase led the way out to his pickup and dropped her suitcase in the tray beside his grocery purchases. He opened the passenger door and then the rear door for her to put Zoe into the infant seat and, while she secured the baby, he drew the tarp back over the rear of the pickup.

Slipping in behind the steering wheel, he twisted around and leaned over to place his laptop on the back seat. He caught Charlie watching him, chewing the full bottom lip he shouldn't be noticing. She smiled, the tip to her lips hesitant, unsure. It had the same effect on him he imagined a bolt of lightning would. Electric, paralyzing, invigorating, hot. And if he didn't stop staring, she'd soon need reassurance he wasn't some weirdo.

"Ready to go?" He smiled back in a way he hoped would ease her nerves. "It's about a half hour drive south on the way to Salmon Prairie. The ranch is called the Triple C."

She closed the rear door and climbed into the seat beside him. Tugging on her seat belt, she blew out a breath. "Okay, tell me more about it."

Chase turned in the direction of the ranch. Beside him,

Charlie twisted her hands. He wanted to still the movement with a touch, but he kept his hands on the wheel instead. A touch like that in a space so small reeked of intimacy. Not a road he wanted to head down while his instincts scrambled for solid ground.

"You have nothing to worry about. You'll be perfectly safe, and you won't be alone. The ranch accommodates up to fifty guests. We're booked up right through until Christmas. My family can be gruff and overbearing at times, but they don't bite. Carter is the cowboy in the family. He loves the ranch."

And shit, he was closer to her in age too. He didn't want to think about his brother stealing this green-eyed girl out from under his nose. He hadn't even touched on Mason yet. The town's bad boy whose reputation stemmed from hiding the pain and guilt that resulted from their youngest brother, Mitch's death. Yet another reason Chase had earned his reputation of mothering, because he'd damn well do anything to protect his siblings from being hurt.

"I feel like an intruder." Her words whispered into the space between them, over the music playing softly on the radio.

An intruder who'd found it necessary to hide in the garage attic. He wanted to know what that was about. "It's a guest ranch. You're my guest."

She smiled, and he'd be lost if he didn't keep reminding himself about the baby and her absent daddy. Hard facts to remember when Charlie's smile made him forget to breathe.

"I feel like I'm getting deeper and deeper in your debt. How do you know I won't walk away with the family heirlooms?"

Excellent question. Telling her he trusted his gut instinct would be a lie. Because his gut instinct screamed trouble in capital letters. Only it wasn't the family heirlooms he was worried about.

DARKNESS COVERED MOST of the road on the way out of town. Lights glittered along the shores of Bigfork Bay. Charlie imagined the warm glow of hearth fires inside the log cabins that lined the shore. Happy families snuggled down for the night with not an ounce of discord in sight. So unlike her own family where power and success drove them forward, where affection was quarantined to occasions like podium wins and sponsorship deals, delivered in handshakes and back-pats rather than hugs and cheek kisses.

Beside her, Chase's capable hands controlled the wheel at a steady pace, in no hurry to get where he wanted to be, the ribbon of road disappearing steadily beneath them through the twin beams of the headlights.

The ticking noise of the turn signal sounded loud in the silence as Chase turned the pickup onto the gravel road that led through the wrought-iron gates of the Triple C. Warm, welcoming light flickered from old-fashioned lanterns on either side of the stone arch that decorated the entrance.

"Nice place." In the center of a circle of tents to her left, a bonfire glowed against a star-studded, black velvet sky. A sky that changed as easily as the moods of a Montana fall.

"Carter runs the guest ranch. He stays in the main house with Dad. Mason and I each have our own cabins, as do Grace and Trinity. But since the girls aren't home much, we rent those out to people who don't want to camp in the tents."

"It must be nice living so close to your family." If only her family had encouraged a tighter-knit relationship, but with the focus on Ronan and his career, she'd been pretty much invisible.

"We're tight, except for Grace. She's the rebel child." He grinned in the dim light of the cab. "She and Carter are twins, but she sees herself as the middle child."

Charlie shrugged. She wouldn't have a clue with only one sibling, but she'd learned how to survive being ignored.

Chase drove past the main ranch house and pulled up outside a smaller log cabin, the porch light burning brightly. He turned off the motor. Silence filled the space between them for a moment. He dropped his hand to his thigh and Charlie followed the movement to where strong muscles stretched the denim tight over his legs. She pushed down the swell of attraction. Why did he have to be so darn *nice*? She'd fallen for charming before and look where it landed her.

From her infant seat in the back, Zoe made little noises as she woke from her motion-induced slumber. The smell of wood smoke drifted into the truck through the air vents.

Charlie looked out at the small group gathered near a bonfire a few yards away, the sound of laughter rippling through the night.

"If you're uncomfortable sharing my cabin, I can stay up at the main house. I'd put you in one of the other cabins, but they're booked up for the season. And I'd hate for you to stay in one of the tents with a baby, even though they have heating."

"I'm not afraid of you." *I'm afraid of myself.*

Six-feet-three of hard-to-resist hunk with arms of corded muscle and a smile that flipped her insides. Chase Calhoun was easy on the eyes. And a true, all round Mr. Nice Guy.

It would be so easy to fall for someone like him, to project all the dreams she'd almost given up on believing in, into the hope for a future with someone to love. Someone who would love her back for who she really was rather than the rebel she was always portrayed as. He pushed open the door of the pickup, the interior light filling the cabin. "Good. Let's get you settled inside. It's cold out here."

Charlie shivered as night air drifted inside the pickup. Sitting out here wouldn't do either of them any good. "Okay." She cast a look at Zoe. At least they'd have a soft, warm bed to sleep in tonight.

Chase walked around the hood of the pickup to open her door. He held out his hand to her, the touch sending tingles of pleasure through her. Over his shoulder, she saw a man walking toward them who could only be his brother. Just as tall with the same shape face and nose, but with his hair hidden under a wide-brimmed hat. Jeans and a western-style shirt under a warm jacket, zipped halfway up, and leather boots that suited his cowboy swagger. His face, as he came into the light, was a picture of surprise and his grin as wide and almost as heart-stopping as his brother's. The Calhouns had been blessed by great genes.

"I thought you went back into town to pick up your *laptop*?"

"I did. It's in the back." Chase smiled as Charlie's feet hit the dirt. He steadied her with a hand at her back. "Right next to the baby. Carter, meet Charlie."

"Ma'am." Carter touched the brim of his hat, tipping it down a little to cover the hint of laughter in bright blue eyes. "Baby, huh? God knows what you'd come home with if we sent you into town for milk."

Chase chuckled, the sound sending shock waves through Charlie's blood, warming it until it settled somewhere below the tie-string waistband of her track pants. "Charlie's the one who ate my chicken salad sandwich and drank all the milk."

"Ah, the refrigerator thief. I'd heard about that. My money was on Mason. So where did he find you hiding?" He winked at Charlie and the tension between her shoulder blades eased.

"In the attic," Chase answered as he opened the back door of the pickup, so Charlie could unclip Zoe from her seat.

Carter stiffened for a moment before he blew out a long whistle and assessed Charlie from head to toe. "The attic, huh? Whoa, I need to go up there more often. I don't suppose there are any more of you hiding up there?"

Charlie laughed, the cowboy's teasing far too charming to take offense to. Besides, it had been a long time since someone had paid her a compliment. "No, only me and a baby." She lifted Zoe out of the pickup.

Chase tucked a blanket around Zoe. "Carter, make yourself useful and bring me one of the portable cribs from the stock room. Zoe's been sleeping in the laundry basket. I think she deserves something a little more comfortable."

Carter shook his head. "Yes, Mother. I'm on it."

Chase's eyes flashed, and he gave his brother a little shove. "Smart-ass."

Carter placed a gentle hand on Charlie's arm. "Don't let him mother you too, okay?"

Charlie cast an uncertain look at Chase.

He removed his brother's hand from her sleeve. "Ignore him. Carter's like an untrained puppy." The smile he delivered turned her knees weak. "This is what happens when we let him off his leash."

Carter laughed, the sound echoing through the night making Zoe whimper. Charlie soothed her as Chase led her into the cabin and closed the door behind them. Warmth surrounded her, seeping into her bones. So much better than the attic. But she couldn't allow herself to get too used to this—the warmth, the banter, the family environment. How long could she hide before reality found her?

Chapter Four

CHASE CURSED CARTER'S teasing. Charlie had retreated into silence, responding only with nods or murmurs. He led her into the living room.

"The guest bedroom is to the right of the stairs leading to the loft. You've got a bathroom down there too. I'd offer you the loft, given your penchant for attics, but it's a little messy up there." He grinned. "Besides, I think you'd prefer to be closer to the kitchen. Great room left and center at the big windows, dining room to the right and kitchen next to it in the corner." He waved a hand at the three living spaces of the open plan cabin. "The porch in the front gives you a great sunrise. The porch out the back gives you a beautiful sunset. Make yourself at home while I bring in your bags and the groceries."

Chase stepped back out the door, off the front porch, and took the short walk to the pickup, only to find his brothers leaning against it. Mason with a foot on the rear bumper and his ass on the tailgate, and Carter leaning on the hood. He ignored them as he reached for the carryall, his laptop, and the groceries from Molly's.

"Nice bag. Pink suits you." Mason pushed off the back

of the pickup and fingered the weave of the bag. "Macy's? Or Walmart?"

"Haven't you kids got anything better to do?" Chase scowled.

"Is this the same girl you rescued at Molly's today?" Carter chipped in, his teasing grin gone. "Is the baby yours?"

Irritation skittered along Chase's nerve ends. "No, the baby isn't mine. Why don't you mind your own business? Haven't you got guests to entertain?"

"Dad's telling them about the possibility of a television series contract for Calhoun Customs." Mason lifted a brown bag of groceries from his arms. "I'll take that. Who's the girl, Mother? Might go inside and introduce myself."

"You boys need to stop calling me that."

"Can't stop it if it's true." Carter nodded in the direction of the cabin. "How do you know she's not a scam artist?"

"Because she had the opportunity to steal a whole lot more than just a chicken sandwich and she didn't. She's in trouble."

"What's her name?" Mason rifled through the contents of the grocery bag.

"Charlie."

"Charlie who?" This from Carter who lifted the laptop from under Chase's arm.

Darn it. Chase raked a hand through his hair. "Just Charlie."

Mason's hand froze halfway to his mouth with a grape between his fingers. "You don't even know her whole name?"

"No. Carter, where are you going with that laptop?" he called as Carter stepped onto the front porch and headed for the front door.

"We're going to Skype-call Trinity. She'll love this. It might make her come home sooner." Carter nodded at the folded portable crib. "And bring that inside with you."

Damn it, it was going to be a long night. Mason pushed past him and followed Carter through the door. Chase slammed the pickup door shut and followed them. He didn't need his brothers gawking, seeing what he'd seen and taking a liking to her in a way that wouldn't be okay with him.

Charlie sat on the floor, legs crossed, with Zoe in her lap, talking quietly to the baby. In the soft lighting, her skin glowed and the smile she shared with Zoe was nothing short of beautiful. Her long, blonde braid hung over her shoulder, just out of reach of the tiny little fist trying to take hold of it. Chase brushed off the ache in his chest and blamed it on hunger. He hadn't even had a meal yet. And beans wouldn't be enough for Charlie either.

She looked up, the relaxed smile fleeing. He could only imagine what she saw. Three grown men, all over six foot with varying degrees of muscle, standing with their big boots planted just the other side of the doorframe.

"The boys helped with the load, but they're leaving now." Chase sent his brothers a stern get-lost look.

Carter walked across the room and squatted beside Charlie, giving Zoe a little wave. "Hey, there."

Zoe pursed her lips and blew him a raspberry which he

returned with enthusiasm.

Mason rolled his eyes. "Get over it." He placed the grocery bag on the kitchen counter and stole another grape. "Hi Charlie, I'm Mason. The good-looking one. The fun one. Not like Chase here. How old's the baby?"

"Mason." Chase kept his voice low but stern, afraid to shout as he normally would in case it made Zoe cry. "Back off."

Charlie sighed. "It's okay. She's three months old."

Carter did the calculations. "Not yours then, Chase. You were in Vegas for SEMA, tied up with that showgirl."

"I was not tied up with anyone other than SEMA officials." Suddenly it felt very important that he stress that fact. "And the showgirl photo-bombed the Instagram post."

"Sure she did." Mason turned to Charlie. "You've got to watch Chase. He's a bit of a player."

Oh, good God, would they ever grow up? "Ignore them, Charlie." He put the porta-crib down with a thump and dropped her carryall a little more gently on the floor next to her. "Are you hungry?"

She looked up at him, her eyes a pool of green, uncertainty clear in their depths.

"A little. But I'd kill for a decent shower first. All I've managed so far were short, quick washes. Would that be okay?"

Chase caught the look Mason sent Carter and lip-read his words. *Bunny boiler.* He shot Mason his final warning look before saying, "Of course. Would you like us to take care of Zoe for you?"

She looked at Zoe who was making noises at Carter. Then she looked back at Chase, fear in her eyes, a tremor in her voice. "*No.* I'll take her with me."

Chase studied her thoughtfully. "She'll be safe here. I'll make sure of it." Had someone threatened her or the baby? Was that why she was on the run? The panic in her eyes was too real.

She shook her head. "No, I'll be quick."

"Charlie, let me take care of her. I won't let her out of my sight, I promise." He put all the power of that promise into his eyes as he searched hers for the root of her fear.

Mason cleared his throat, drawing Chase's attention. *Ah, shit.* He looked at his brothers who eyed him back with keen interest. He wished he could wipe the smirks off their faces.

"No problem for you, isn't that right, Chase? Mother here didn't earn his nickname for nothing. He's done it lots of times before," Mason offered.

"Practically raised us all himself. Hope he remembers how to change a diaper though. Trinity's almost twenty-five. And Mitch—" Carter's words cut to silence as he eased up off his haunches. "How about I go get us some meat off that spit roast and bring it over?"

The teasing light died in Mason's eyes. "I'll go too. Bring some bread. And stuff." He brushed past Carter, shoulder-bumping him hard.

As he walked past, Chase gripped his shoulder and squeezed. He hated the weight of guilt his brother carried for something that wasn't his fault. Mason would never let Mitch's ghost rest. "Good idea, guys."

When the door closed behind them, he turned back to Charlie. "They're harmless. I promise."

She nodded. "I have a brother too. He's not quite as nice as yours are."

Chase walked over and sat down next to her, leaning his back against the sofa. "If you look in the drawers in the guest room, you'll find some clean clothes in there. Stuff we bought for Trinity over the years and she's never worn."

Charlie placed her hand on his arm, the skin warm on his, a faint scent of baby powder clinging to her. "Thank you, Chase." Her green gaze met his. "I'll pay you back, I promise."

He covered her hand with his. "You don't have to. But, Charlie, if you need a friend to talk to, you can trust me. My brothers might be a bit of a handful, but they're trustworthy too. So, if you can't talk to me or my dad, go to one of them for help."

She leaned closer for a moment, hesitating before pulling back and dragging her hand out from under his. He could feel reluctance and uncertainty vibrate between them as she debated his offer.

"Thank you. I'll take that shower now." Then she passed Zoe over into his arms. "I'm trusting you with the most precious treasure in my life. Please keep her safe. I won't be long."

"Take as long as you need." Surprised, he could even

find his voice, he watched her stand and walk through the arch into the tiny hallway that led to the guest bedroom and bathroom. Then he looked down at the baby in his arms, and his heart melted a little more.

CHARLIE LEANED HER head against the cool tiles in the bathroom and willed her heart to stop pounding so hard. Lordy, she'd have to be careful around that man. His thoughtfulness and caring nature could be so easy to fall for. He'd taken a risk by inviting her into his home with little more than her word as security. But he had a strong family to support him, a luxury she lacked.

She stripped off her clothes and studied herself in the mirror. When the truth came out about who she was, would the big, strong Calhouns shy away? Would their perfect, happy family be tainted by the black hearts of hers? But running away again wouldn't help her the same way it would if she stayed and found her feet. So, if she wanted to make a go of this new life and keep her child, she'd have to discourage any intimate contact with Chase. She turned on the shower faucet and tested the water before stepping under the spray.

Voices filtered through the closed door, deep and loud. In her heart she knew Chase could be trusted. His brothers had respect for him, irrespective of their teasing. It was there in the way they'd surrounded him, clearly protective as he'd arrived home with a stranger on his arm. The Calhouns were smart. They'd figure out who she was hiding from sooner or later, and she'd rather come clean with them first.

She turned off the water, stepped out of the cubicle and toweled herself dry. Slipping into a pair of track pants and clean T-shirt, she tugged on a hoodie she'd found in the drawer in her room. It fitted a little snug across the chest, but she could deal with that. A quick brush of her hair, and she twisted it back into a braid. Taking a deep breath, she opened the door to face the people who'd given her refuge.

Three men sat on bar chairs at the kitchen counter while Chase soothed Zoe over his shoulder. She gurgled happy noises while the men laughed and talked around her. Silence descended in the room as Chase looked up. The three men eyed his face before turning on their chairs.

Marty smiled warmly. Mason sent her a flirty look. Carter's easy grin tugged at his lips.

And Chase. Oh, Lordy. The hand cupping Zoe's back was almost as big as her baby. There was something ridiculously heartwarming about the man cradling her child, as if he was born to it and not minding the task at all.

She crossed the wooden floor of the cabin, for the first time not feeling like she was doing the walk of shame. If it had been her father and brother sitting on those chairs, they'd be judging her every step.

Marty's eyes narrowed on her, his gaze searching, as if he was trying to peel back the lid on a box of old memories. "Welcome to the Triple C, Charlie."

"Thank you," she murmured as she reached out her arms for Zoe.

Chase walked around the counter to meet her, easing the baby off his shoulder, smiling as she protested. "She was quite happy listening to talk of horsepower and transmissions." He cradled her in the crook of one arm and tickled her belly over the fleecy all-in-one pajama jumpsuit. "I think she might be getting hungry though." He pointed to the wet patch of dribble Zoe had left on his shoulder. "She's been sucking on her fist."

Charlie inhaled the scent of everything Chase. Something fresh and woodsy, layers of man and fresh country air, untainted by the smell of burning rubber, grease and racing fuel.

"It's about time for a feed. If you'll excuse me?" A little too early for one but being near him made her hands itch to touch. To see if he was as solid as he looked, to feel the heat that radiated from him under her palms.

"Before you go, Charlie ... How about you show us some of your designs? Since we're all here now, why wait until tomorrow as planned?" Marty's words hung awkwardly in the air for a moment before Charlie's gaze shot to Chase.

He shrugged. "I saw your sketch pad in the attic. It was open on the blanket next to you. The little I saw was impressive. You can save the full portfolio for later, but I think Dad would like the work I saw tonight."

Her heart beat a little faster. The chance had come to prove herself. "I did graphic artwork in marketing, but my passion lies in design."

"Hand it over then, girl. Passion is what we're looking for." Marty smiled encouragingly at her.

Charlie's heart lodged in her throat. "Sure." She pulled the sketch pad out of the carryall and placed it on the kitchen counter next to Marty. "They're only rough. They still need color and touching up."

Marty's hand hovered over the cover of her tattered sketch pad, the shake in his fingers a jerky, uncontrolled movement. He peeled back the cover to study the artwork.

Charlie took a moment to study him. A big man, as handsome as his sons, except with the wisdom of age etched into his face. This was how Chase would look in thirty or so years. Under a mop of sandy hair, streaked with gray, kind blue eyes raised to meet hers.

A smile spread his lips as he revealed the sketch. "Son, I think you're going to like this," he said, looking at Carter.

Charlie waited, hugging Zoe close, as he pushed the pad along the counter in front of Mason and Carter. She looked up and caught Chase's gaze on her, his expression unreadable. Doubt, fear, apprehension tumbled together in her stomach.

"Like it? I love it. You're a genius, Charlie." Carter smiled broadly.

Charlie released her breath. "The moment I saw the Chevy, I knew what it needed." Excitement fired her imagination, her vision tumbling out into words. "Power in the horses galloping across the sides. Strong hand-brushed strokes to emphasize the outlines. A mare and a stallion. Satin black and rich chestnut. The Triple C logo kicked up by the rear hooves against a mountain background in hazy shades, muted greens and muddy browns so the horses pop in 3-D."

"You gave the sketch life, girl. I can't wait to see the finished result." Marty waved her over. "Come over here and tell me more."

Zoe settled in against her, not yet hungry enough to fuss, relaxing as the tension released from Charlie's shoulders. If it had been her father, he would have insisted on digital imaging, denying her the satisfaction of putting her own artistic signature on the finished product. "No decals. Decals deteriorate over time. They fade to ugly and then you start again. I'm thinking airbrush on a hand-drawn template to make it real and personal. Art rather than marketing. Eye-catching rather than standard mass-manufacturing style."

Marty nodded. "The best way. That's how I'd do it too. Now that I've seen your work, I think we can talk business."

"Sir, it would be an honor to work with you. I really want this job, if you'll give me the chance." Charlie shuffled her feet. "But I can't give you work references." *Please don't let him withdraw his offer.*

She caught the look that passed between the three brothers as their father continued to study her thoughtfully. Mason's smirk met Carter's eye-roll while Chase's face remained expressionless.

"Why not?" Chase stepped toward her, hands on hips,

feet apart. Not threatening, just there—a solid brick wall waiting for her answer.

Zoe squirmed against her, and Charlie ran a soothing hand over her baby's downy head. "My previous ... employer ... and I parted on bad terms."

Marty's eyes narrowed. "How bad?"

Darn it, she couldn't lie to him, not with Chase's eyes piercing a hole in her soul. "Real bad." If she blew her chance here with the Calhouns, she'd have to move on, and she didn't have a plan B yet.

"Anyone else we can contact?" Chase kept his gaze locked on hers, a deep sea of blue that could so easily make her spill everything.

"I've only ever had one employer."

Marty eased off his seat. "Stand down, Chase. You're like some damn guard dog waiting to snap at a piece of butcher's meat. The girl's not exactly a wanted criminal now, is she?"

"But we don't know that, do we, Dad?" Mason interjected.

"I can assure you I'm not."

Marty sighed. "How bad is your situation, girl?"

Charlie looked past Chase at his father. "I need a job, a place to stay, and someone I can trust to take care of Zoe while I'm at work. Please, Mr. Calhoun, it's just that I'd prefer you don't approach my previous employer. He wouldn't give me a good reference." And when her father finally caught up with her, he'd make her suffer the consequences—publicly, in the most humiliating way he could find. "I'd rather prove myself to you."

"What would you like from us then?"

"I'll work on Carter's truck for a roof over our heads and a bed to sleep in. If you like what I do, we can negotiate a wage and then I can afford my own accommodation."

By then she would have had time to establish herself, to prove to herself she could do the job, earn a living to take care of herself and her daughter. That she could stand alone outside the framework of the family business and follow her own course in life.

"What about Zoe?" Marty asked.

"I'd budgeted for daycare or a babysitter when I applied for the job in Kalispell. If you can recommend someone here in Bigfork who provides that service, I'd appreciate it."

All looks zoomed in on Chase. "Oh, hell no. Wait a minute—"

"Makes perfect sense. You're the one with the office." Carter slapped his brother's shoulder.

"And with your mothering skills—" Mason grinned as Chase shot him a filthy look.

"It makes sense for Zoe to be where her mom is. We raised two baby girls and four boys in the garage, and you all turned out just fine. No reason we can't raise another." Marty's tone allowed for no argument. "Airbrushing takes place in the booth, Charlie. No health risks for her if she stays in the garage while you work. I'll be honest, girl, I like what I see in those sketches. I think you'll be a good fit here at Calhoun Customs. Now, I don't know what kind of trouble you're in and be assured, you can ask us for help with it, but I don't want to invite discord to my doorstep. Understood?"

Charlie nodded. "I understand, sir. I don't want any trouble either." And, damn it, she'd do everything she could to make sure trouble stayed as far east of the Montana border as possible.

Chapter Five

TROUBLE. CHASE SETTLED Zoe into the porta-crib he'd set up in his office. Outside the window, Charlie leaned over the fender of Carter's '57 Chevy marking out the lines of her design with tape. And damned if she didn't look good doing it.

In the three days since he'd taken her home, he'd gotten used to having the two girls around. The smell of baby powder in the air, Charlie's shoes in the mudroom out back, Zoe's clothing in the drier. The cabin no longer felt empty. A dangerous sign of trouble.

Zoe protested in the porta-crib, rubbing her eyes. Over-tired. He picked her up again, placed her against his shoulder and held her there with one hand. It blew him away that she was so tiny; his hand almost completely covered her back. He used the other hand to Skype-call Trinity. He'd put off the conversation for long enough while they'd ironed out the details of having Charlie on trial in the garage. Charlie, whose last name he still didn't know, and she danced around telling them. He waited while Trinity's number rang, then her face appeared on the screen.

"Hey, Mother." Trinity stood with her racing suit

stripped to her waist, the fire-retardant skins she wore under it hugging her slim shape.

Chase groaned. "Not you too?"

Trinity sipped from her bottle of water. "You caught me on a break. I got pole position for the Delaware 400. Hurry, they'll want me at the board to dissect the qualifying round any minute now."

"Proud of you, girl. I guess now's not a good time to talk to you about Dad?"

Trinity frowned. "Now's as good a time as any. What's up with Dad?"

Chase sighed and leaned forward, bringing Zoe down off his shoulder and settling her into the crook of his arm.

Trinity gasped. "Oh. My. God. Chase Calhoun, is that a baby? What have you been up to in that town?"

Chase grinned. "Sounds like a question more suited to Mason than me." He waved to Paige, Trinity's mechanic and Mason's ex-girlfriend, who appeared in the frame next to his sister. "Hey, Paige." He saw the sad look on the girl's face. "The baby isn't Mason's either."

The two girls looked at each other. "Whose is it then? Not Carter's, surely?" Trinity peered into the screen to try and get a closer look. "Grace would have known if it was, being his twin and all."

"Settle down. She's not any of ours."

"Good. Because the only one left would be Dad." She wrinkled her nose. "And that would just be … eww."

"Listen up, brat." His tone softened with affection for

the baby of the family. His favorite sister. Not that he'd ever let Grace find out. It would give her yet another reason to butt heads with him. Another excuse to stay away. "Dad hasn't been well lately. I took him to the doctor and we had some tests done."

Trinity's smile slipped from her face. "Oh no. Is he going to be okay, Chase?"

"He has Parkinson's, honey. It's in the early stages and we are doing everything we can for him, but you know how Dad hates taking medication."

"Well that just sucks."

"Pretty much."

"How long before … you know …"

Chase didn't want to think about how long they had left with him before the disease stole his control. "It's creeping in like a dark and dirty shadow right now. But once it takes hold, who knows. Will you be coming home at the end of the season?"

"Yeah, I wanted to talk to you about that. Brant has sold the team to some guy in San Francisco. Looks like he's got his own drivers and pit crew. Which could leave Paige and me on the sidelines. I was thinking of retiring at the end of the season."

"Sounds like perfect timing. Dad wants you to come home, but he doesn't want you to sacrifice your career for it."

"What will we do there, though?"

"Dad's going to need help once he starts losing mobility.

Mason's already doing some of the work, in between helping Carter at the ranch. We could use Paige's expertise. Yours too."

"I haven't swung a wrench in a long time, Chase." Trinity grimaced. "And I'm not sure Paige would want to be anywhere near Mason. But I'll work on it, okay?"

"Great. Let me know."

"Okay. Gotta go. They're calling me to the board. So, whose baby is it?"

Chase smiled. "Charlie's."

Trinity frowned. "Charlie?"

"Our newly hired graphics artist. She's new in town and doing a trial run on Carter's pickup. She does good work."

"Really?" Trinity drew the word out and ended it on a mischievous chuckle. "You make a good baby-daddy. Is there a Mr. Charlie on the scene?"

Chase frowned. "None of my business. Or yours, brat. Get to work now so you can hurry up and come home."

She blew him a kiss. "See you, Mother."

He blew one back. "Stay safe out there, okay?"

"I always am. The last race will be for Mitch. I'm bringing a car home with me, so hang on to your Charlie, because I'm gonna need some good graphics."

His Charlie. That shouldn't make his stomach flip or his heart rate increase, but it did. He looked out the window to where she worked, deep in concentration. Then down at Zoe, content in his arms, her tiny little hand fisted in his shirt, stealing another piece of his heart with every day that went by. Whatever secrets Charlie was hiding, he almost wished they wouldn't surface any time soon. But that would be irresponsible thinking if her secrets had the power to harm his family.

"I'll see what I can do, princess. Go now." He waved her away and offered a thumbs-up to Paige, who stood fiddling with a wrench in the background, turning it over and over in her hands. No doubt the thoughts would be doing the same thing in her mind at the mention of Mason's name. Another old Band-Aid he'd like to rip off, so everyone's scars could heal.

"I'm gone." Trinity pressed her lips to the screen. "That's for the baby, not you. Bye."

The screen blanked out as his sister ended the call. Chase smiled. It would be damn good if he could get the whole family home again. He scrolled down his list of contacts and hit dial on Grace's number. It rang out. He'd try again tomorrow.

"Aunty Grace is no doubt somewhere out in the Arizona desert on that Harley of hers. She'll be a tough one to convince. It won't be easy to bring that vagabond home."

Zoe answered with a hum and blew spit bubbles at him. Chase laughed and wiped the drool off her chin with her bib.

"I thought she'd be asleep." Charlie stood in the doorway with her shoulder against the frame, feet crossed at the ankles, her expression blank.

At the sound of her mom's voice, Zoe whimpered. Chase stood and walked around the desk toward Charlie. "She was a bit fussy still. I thought she might settle if I hold her."

Charlie straightened and held out her arms to take the baby. "You'll spoil her. It's what all the books say."

Chase grimaced as he handed Zoe over. She curled toward her mother, snuggling in. "The books aren't always right. She's a good baby."

"She is."

A warm smile spread on Charlie's lips, the sight of which grabbed his heart and squeezed. Oh, he was in all kinds of trouble here. He'd be better off not getting too close to his mystery guests. He couldn't afford to lose his heart. He should step out of her space now that he'd handed the baby over. That would be the smart thing to do. Apparently, he wasn't as smart as he thought he was. Certainly not around Charlie.

CHARLIE SHOULD BACK away from him, but his body generated a comfortable warmth in the space between them. Strong arms crossed over his chest, the size of the muscles in his forearms suggesting he did more around the garage than just marketing and finances. She understood why his brothers teased him about being motherly. Chase had a way of making everyone feel safe and cared for.

"How's the design coming along?" Chase offered her a smile that could melt chocolate.

"Taping it out is the hardest part. Once I start airbrushing, things should move along nicely."

"Carter's pretty happy with the sketch."

She'd added the colors, blended the lines and created a flow across the page that encompassed the Calhoun's logo. A mixture of landscape and horsepower, strength and presence—everything that united the Calhoun family. "I can't wait to get started. It'll look even better on the Chevy." Marty had chosen Dusk Pearl for the duco on the body, giving her the perfect canvas to work with. No computer graphics in sight. Only pure, invigorating, exciting, passionate art. She flashed Chase a smile that encompassed all that. "I won't let you down. I won't waste this opportunity."

"I have faith in you, Charlie." He lifted a hand as if to touch her face, hesitated then shoved both hands in his pockets instead.

Disappointment flooded her even though she shouldn't want to feel this attraction to him. Perhaps her father was right. Maybe her brother's taunts were on target. *Charlotte the Harlot.* Unoriginal, yet no less hurtful. *You'd do anything for attention, wouldn't you, Charlotte? Even bring disgrace to the family.* Easy thing for the star of the family to say when he'd captured and held the spotlight all his life while she'd been pushed out in the cold in the shadows of his brilliance, her own talents ignored.

She hugged Zoe tighter for just a moment before holding her out to Chase. "I'd better get back to work."

Chase studied her steadily as he took Zoe in his arms. "What are you running from, Charlie?"

"Myself. But I'm not running anymore."

"You're still hiding."

Charlie's heart danced around a misstep. "Not hiding. Buying time."

"Time for what?"

Time to grow, to put down roots, find the happy place where she could raise her daughter in a warm and loving environment, and fulfill her dreams outside of her brother's shadow, away from the stark, cold, controlled environment of TRJ Racing.

The rub of Chase's thumb across her frown drew her from her thoughts. "Whatever trouble you're in, we can help you."

Pride, stubbornness, and sheer determination chased through her. She'd made the decision to run away and take control of her life. She wouldn't rely on strangers to do for her what she had to do herself. "I'm not in any trouble. I just have things I need to take care of. And that's on me. Zoe's almost asleep. She'll settle now. I'll get back to work."

"I'll leave it, Charlie. For now. But sooner or later, I hope you'll trust me enough to tell me."

Chase turned away from her. He placed Zoe gently in the porta-crib and pulled the blanket up to her shoulders. She whimpered, and he soothed her back then he straightened and moved back to his desk.

She watched him for a moment. He knew she hadn't left. The awareness was there in his movements. He dragged a hand through his short blond hair making it stick up every which way then ran his palm around the edge of his jaw before pulling a folder toward him and flicking through it.

With a sigh of regret, Charlie pushed away from the doorframe and went back into the garage. She hated keeping secrets, avoiding the truth, but trust came hard when it had been betrayed so often in the past. It was enough that the Calhouns had given her a chance to prove herself. She couldn't let them fight her battles too.

Picking up a roll of tape, she moved toward the fender of the Chevy. Marty leaned on the other side, his head under the hood as he waited for his hand to stop shaking so he could torque the spark plugs he'd put in the motor.

"Everything okay?" He looked up as she approached.

Charlie nodded. "Fine."

Marty continued to study her face. "Don't look fine to me." He placed the torque wrench on top of the block. "Come with me. I want to show you something."

Charlie looked at him uncertainly. "I should get on with the design."

"It'll only take a minute," he reassured her. "I want you to understand what makes Chase tick."

"With all due respect to you and your family, it's none of my business, Marty. I appreciate this opportunity you've given me and the place to stay, but it's better I don't understand any of you."

"I'd ask why not, but I already know the answer. Trust takes a long time to earn when you've been hurt before, Charlie. We Calhouns know that more than the rest." He stepped around the front of the pickup and held out his hand. "Come along. I think it's important you know what you're dealing with here." He gestured toward the showroom and held out his hand to her.

After a moment's hesitation, Charlie took his out-stretched hand. Warm fingers closed firmly around hers in a way her father's never had. Reassuring, comforting, encouraging. She let him tug her through the door into the expanse of the showroom where fall had started to strip the trees of their leaves outside the vast windows. He led her past the shape in the shadowy corner draped in a soft, nylon cover.

"What's under there?"

Marty's eyes clouded over for a moment. "Mason's old pickup. We need to fix it. One day."

"A restoration?"

Sadness etched his voice. "Accident damage."

"Why keep it in here?"

"Because Mason won't let it be moved." He tugged on her hand gently. "That's a story for another day. Come on."

Curiosity eased away the bad feeling that curled in her gut as she followed him over to a gallery of portraits on the far wall of the showroom. Marty stopped at the start of the gallery and pointed to a picture in the top row on the far-left corner.

"That's me and my wife, Nora. I'd won my very first NASCAR race. She was so proud of me. Chase was only three months old. Same age as your Zoe. Ten years later, she died."

The ache of his loss came through clearly in his words, making Charlie's heart clench. "I'm so sorry."

He nodded. "She was the most beautiful girl in the world to me. Inside and out. She'd do anything for anyone, even if it cost her. Chase has that same caring nature she had." He moved on to the next portrait. "This is two years later. By then I held the title of champion. That's Chase, and the baby is Mason."

Charlie studied the two-year-old Chase. A sweet, innocent face, looking up at his mother and baby brother with a cheeky grin. The same smile he still had years later. She pointed to the next photo. "Who's that?"

Marty chuckled as he studied the portrait. Chase and Mason stood between their parents, while Marty and his wife each held a bundle. One pink and one blue. "Our celebration surprises. The twins, Carter and Grace came just over two years after Mason. Not what Nora had planned for but was happy to receive anyway. Nora doted on the children. She was a great mom. Born to it, I always said." He dragged a rag from his pocket and dabbed at his eyes and nose before shoving it away again. "Chase wasn't much more than four at the time, but he took a step up to help his mom as best he could. By the time young Mitch came along three or so years later, Nora was a full-time mom, so she didn't travel with me around the circuit anymore. It wasn't the same without her and the children by my side, cheering me on."

Charlie smiled. How awesome it would have been to have two parents who loved each other so much that the one without the other was incomplete. One day, she hoped to find a love like that. "How much longer did you race for?"

Sadness etched into his features once more as he pointed to the last portrait in the row. "I gave it away the day Nora died. I should have been there, but I missed my flight home from Daytona Beach. I'd been invited to a party after the race. Got a little drunk on the success of winning against Tony Jackson."

Charlie hissed in a breath at the mention of her father's name, her heart pounding. "I'm sorry."

Her father had never been good at losing. She could only imagine the scene he might have caused as a young, hot-headed racing driver. Most likely close to the ones her brother, Ronan, caused when he lost. There'd be accusations of cheating, race-setting, investigations into builds and pit stops while her father searched for excuses for his loss and someone else to pin the blame on.

"When I arrived home, they'd taken her to the hospital. In those days, we lived in the attic above the garage. I'd put up drywall to make rooms for the children, but we still used the kitchen and bathroom downstairs. Nora took a tumble down the stairs to the attic that night which resulted in her going into labor. She was almost full term. Trinity survived, but Nora didn't make it." He turned to Charlie, tears glittering unashamedly in his eyes. "Chase was the one who found her. She was bleeding badly. He called an ambulance then fetched Molly from across the road to help. He stayed behind to look after his brothers and sister while Molly rode with Nora in the ambulance. And he's been looking out for them ever since while living in his own personal hell. Chase thinks he's responsible, that his mother's death was his fault."

"But that's—"

"Crazy? Yes. But, you see, Charlie, both my boys are afraid to face the truth, to step outside of themselves and see that sometimes in life things happen beyond your control. That sometimes fate has a plan and it doesn't always make sense at the time. Sometimes never. The kind of plan that brought you to hide out here in Bigfork. Do you believe in fate, young Charlie?"

She thought back to her first night in the attic. The peace and comfort she'd found there. In a home she now knew was once filled with the happiness of family. "If you'd asked me that question twelve months ago, I would have denied it. It sounds so fanciful saying it out loud, but would you believe me if I said I'd felt drawn to the attic the moment I saw it? That I felt someone guiding me to it, and a kind of peace when I found it?"

Marty smiled. "I'd believe it. If Nora were alive, she'd have done exactly that. She was a beautiful, generous soul, my Nora." He looked up at a group photo, labeled with the date and location of the NASCAR race, and tapped it with his finger. "See this girl here?" He turned the force of his sharp blue gaze on hers. "She reminds me of you."

Charlie swallowed as she looked at her mother in the photograph. A smiling, happy young wife. A beautiful, warm, elated young woman far removed from the ice queen Charlie had grown up knowing. She chewed her lip.

Marty's hand came down and he patted her arm. "I don't know why you're hiding, girl, but I know who you are. Don't you think my son deserves to know too?"

Chapter Six

CHASE TAPPED HIS fingers against the steering wheel as silence filled the cabin of the pickup on the drive home. Marty, riding shotgun, kept his eyes on the road. Charlie sat in the back with Zoe, staring out the window at the passing landscape while Zoe made happy baby noises, oblivious of the tension.

He had no idea what to say to Charlie. The tension that had sprung up between them earlier had stretched through the day. What exactly had his father told her when he'd taken her into the showroom that had her so lost in thought now?

Chase pulled up next to the main ranch house and waited for his father to climb out. "See you in the morning, Dad. Call me if you need anything."

"Sure, Son." He stuck his head back in. "See you in the morning, Charlie. You did good work today." Marty closed the door and waved through the window.

Chase waited until Carter opened the door for his dad before he pulled away to drive the short distance to his cabin.

Watching Charlie work was almost as bewitching as watching her interact with Zoe. She'd moved with the grace of a ballet dancer as she'd progressed from the front fender to the rear tailgate on the Chevy. He's seen her stretch the kinks from her spine, shake the stiffness from her fingers holding the paintbrush as she'd outlined her work. He'd meant it when he'd said they wouldn't let her go easily, whatever secrets she was keeping.

He parked the pickup under the lean-to next to the cabin, shut off the motor and got out. Charlie was out the door before he could open it for her, reaching for Zoe. He'd never meant to hurt her with his questions. In the tight space between the cabin wall and the pickup, he waited for her to squeeze past him, her back to him, their bodies touching. He wanted to stop her, to apologize but, with the wind cutting in through the gaps and touching them with icy fingers, his apology would have to wait until they were inside.

Chase gathered up his laptop and scarf from the back seat and closed the door. On the porch, he slipped off his boots and held them in his hand as he followed Charlie inside. She dropped her carryall onto the sofa and balanced Zoe on her hip. He pushed the front door closed with his foot, placed his laptop on the table and his boots on the rack. Charlie's shoes lay discarded on the floor next to the door. He picked them up and put them next to his.

She looked so small and vulnerable in the open space of the cabin with her scarf around her neck, her beanie slightly askew and Zoe in her arms. And he had nothing to say that wouldn't sound like mothering.

"So, what would you like for dinner?" Mothering. He

tried again. "Is it warm enough in here for you and Zoe or should I light a fire?" Yeah, mothering again. He could almost hear Mason's laughter.

A smile touched Charlie's lips. "How about I sort Zoe out with a bath and a feed, and then I'll cook dinner?"

And what the hell would he do with himself until then? He slipped off his coat and hung it on the coatrack. He'd had the same routine since he was ten. Sort out the kids, cook dinner, clean up, shower, and settle in for some sports on ESPN or maybe a movie on one of the other channels. Chase looked from the kitchen to the television and tried to visualize the contents of his freezer. What would she even cook?

"A fire would be nice though. And a cup of tea." Charlie stepped forward and placed a hand on his arm.

Warmth flowed through him at her brief touch.

"You're good at taking care of people. Maybe it's time someone did something nice for you." She hitched Zoe higher on her hip and supported her back with her hand.

Chase dropped his gaze to his socks and wished she'd touch him again. "I don't know any other way. Taking care of people is what I've done my whole life."

"That's a strength, not a failing. If the people in my world were more like you, I wouldn't need to be here."

There was a thought that sent a chill up his spine. He couldn't imagine life without Charlie, and she'd only been in his for less than a week. "Tell me about them?"

"How about I share some of my secrets over dinner and a

glass of wine? Now that Zoe is taking a bottle, I can have a glass without being worried about the alcohol affecting her."

He lifted a hand to cup her cheek, her fair skin almost translucent against his. "Sounds great."

He rubbed the silky smoothness of her cheekbone with his thumb and wondered what she'd do if he kissed her. Just a small touch of his lips to hers, to explore this … thing … between them. The tug of attraction, the need to take it one step further to see if it grew, to test the question of the right or wrong of it. Green eyes met his, full of questions and a touch of regret.

She covered his hand with hers, pressed a kiss to his palm and moved out of his reach. "Don't make me fall in love with you, Chase. The cost is too high. For both of us."

Then she and Zoe were gone, and he was left standing alone, staring at the empty space she left behind. Dragging a hand through his hair, he walked over to the kitchen and set the kettle to boil on the stove. The front door of the cabin opened, and Mason breezed in, blowing on his hands.

"Colder than a hag with frostbite out there. What's for dinner?"

"Keep your voice down. Charlie's trying to settle Zoe."

Mason pulled a face. "Sorry. I forgot." He looked at the empty gas grids on the stove and headed for the refrigerator. "Formula, pureed apple, vanilla custard … what the fu … dge? Where's the man food?"

"Try your own cabin," suggested Chase, dryly.

"Not as much fun as yours." He pulled out a jar of pickles. "Seriously?"

Chase took them from him and placed them on the kitchen counter with a thump. "From Molly."

"You always were her favorite."

Chase frowned. "You are too. So are the others. Just ask her."

Mason closed the refrigerator door and leaned back against the counter. "I haven't been the favorite in this town for a long time."

Chase pushed away from watching the kettle, waiting for it to boil. He bit back a sigh as he glanced at the calendar on the wall and the big red circle around the date. A night when they remembered the chunk of their hearts they'd lost. "It wasn't anyone's fault."

"You tell the town that. I know you've got guests, but are you coming up the hill for the memorial service tonight?"

"I'll be there." Their usual ritual. They'd make their way along the short distance to the family cemetery, take candles and say prayers for their mother and brother, both of whom had died too young. Then he and Mason would stay behind, get blind drunk and try to forget for another year while Carter and Dad pretended not to wait to see them home safely.

"Would be nice if Grace and Trinity were here."

"They'll come home when they're ready." Chase shoulder-bumped his brother.

Mason blinked and squeezed his eyes closed, pinching the bridge of his nose with his fingers. "I know. I miss the brats. And Dad? What are we going to do about his Parkinson's? It sucks to see him like this."

"There's not a whole lot we can do except take one day at a time and appreciate every moment we have left together. Go on now. I'll be up after dinner."

"So, you're telling me I'm stuck with my instant chicken soup?"

"You could go to Carter's?"

Mason wrinkled his nose. "He's on a health kick. He thinks if he feeds Dad those organic shakes it will make him better."

Chase grinned. "Who knows, it might?"

"If it doesn't kill him first," Mason scoffed. "Meat. A man must have meat. Rich in iron and vitamins. Red raw in the middle, seared on the outside. I think I might cook myself a steak." He caught Chase in a headlock and kissed the top of his head before releasing him. "See you, Mother."

Then he was gone in a whirlwind of energy that hid the scars that festered inside him. A mountain of a man with a lost boy hiding inside. Chase hated that after five years since Mitch's death, Mason still carried his brother's ghost on his shoulders the way he had the real boy many years ago.

CHARLIE STEPPED INTO the living area of the cabin, her heart heavy. It had been hard not to overhear the brothers' conversation when the cabin was so small, and Mason was such a larger-than-life character.

She stood close enough to appreciate the hard contours of Chase's shoulders, broad chest, and hips. He'd removed the layers of clothing in the warmth of the cabin, and all that lay between them was the denim of his jeans and the worn softness of cotton. She reached out to him, her fingers curling around thick biceps exposed by the sleeves of his black T-shirt.

Charlie wished she could erase the sadness in his eyes. It didn't seem fair that a family with such a strong bond should lose two good people. Yet they had. Their mother had been a warm, loving mom. So far removed from Charlie's, who preferred her creature comforts over her children and never showed affection in case it ruined her cosmetics or Chanel suits. How often had she wished that things could be different? What had happened to the woman in the photograph that hung on the wall of the garage?

The haunted look, the pinch of his lips, the frown that hinted at the turmoil in his thoughts—it tugged at her heart. Charlie lifted her hand. The stubble on his jaw caressed her palm. "Everything okay?"

He nodded. "You heard?"

Charlie ran her hand from his cheek down his arm. "Yes. Your dad told me about your mom. I'm sorry. It must have been hard for you."

Chase sighed, his hands moving to caress her back absently. "Not as hard as it was for Dad to lose Mom. She was his anchor, his everything. And tonight, it's the anniversary of Mitch's accident. In some ways, Dad lost two sons that day because Mason has never been the same since."

"The pickup under cover in the corner of the garage?"

He nodded. "It's been five years since Mitch died. Mason won't let us move it outside. He's not ready to let it go or fix it."

Charlie slipped her arms around his waist and laid her cheek against his chest. "Oh, Chase ... and now your dad too."

He drew her closer. She closed her eyes and held him tightly, willing him to feel the comfort and compassion in her heart. She wanted to ask what had happened, but it felt like an intrusion, and she was still a stranger in their circle.

"Life is full of challenges, Charlie. It's how we deal with them that matters." His arms dropped from around her and she released him reluctantly.

"It's still not easy," she said as he stepped away and the air between them cooled to room temperature.

"No, but we will get through it." He rubbed a hand over his face. "I should warn you that part of this ritual tonight means getting very, very drunk. I can sleep at Mason's or Carter's. I might not make it up the stairs to my room. It wouldn't be fair on you and Zoe."

"This is your home, Chase. We'll be fine. Noise doesn't worry Zoe and at least I'll know you're okay when you come home."

He looked at her in a way that made her toes curl in her socks from the heat it generated. Then he turned and walked the short distance to the kitchen to make her tea. Charlie followed him. She pulled out saucepans and ingredients, already familiar with the contents of the refrigerator and cabinet pantry. Pasta and chili sauce, the perfect meal for a man who had to brave the cold of a Montana night.

Charlie opened the refrigerator and searched for green peppers, fresh garlic and chili. She'd promised him her secrets over dinner, but she couldn't add to his burden now. Not when he had his own demons to face. "Will you tell me what happened to Mitch?" She closed the refrigerator door and carried her ingredients over to the sink to rinse them off.

Chase lifted a mug from a cupboard shelf and dropped a tea bag into it. "It's no secret. And while the years in between have allowed the rumors to settle, there are still a few out there who don't mind raising them again when it suits them. Mason loved speed and handling. Racing is in our blood whether we want it or not. I've put my passion into building this business, but Mason, Trinity and Grace have racing fuel in their veins."

Placing the vegetables on a chopping board, Charlie carried them over to the kitchen countertop. She could relate. Her father and brother lived and breathed the adrenaline that drove the race circuit. "That's what has made the Calhoun brand an international brand name."

"That and the errors we've made along the way. Mason was parading his new pickup truck around town the day Mitch died. It was raining that day." He paused as if to listen for the patter of raindrops on the cabin roof. "Mitch was on his way home from town, drenched from the rain. Mason stopped to give him a lift, but he had Paige in the front of the pickup and he didn't want Mitch intruding in their space."

"Paige?" Charlie set a saucepan on the range, filled it with hot water from the kettle and lit the gas under it to bring the water back to the boil. Then she set about quickly chopping the vegetables for the sauce while she waited for the answer that took a while to come.

"His girlfriend at the time and Trinity's best friend still today. She's on Trinity's pit crew. He told Mitch to climb in the back of the pickup and take shelter under the tarp. Mason was young, stupid, in love. Flexing his manhood instead of his brain. He took a bend too sharply, the tail end of the pickup fishtailed and he lost control. Hit a tree." Chase cleared his throat over a crack in his voice. "Mitch was thrown from the back of the pickup. They found him three yards away from the crash site. He didn't stand a chance."

Charlie paused the opening a can of kidney beans, horror sending shivers through her blood. "Poor Mitch." She reached for Chase's hand and found it shaking, so she curled her fingers around his and squeezed comfort into them.

"Mason was devastated. He blamed himself. We did too for a while and so did the town. Gossip spread fast. Some were comforting and forgiving. Others not so much. Some people gave Mason a hard time over the accident. It sent him into a downward spiral so bad we had him on suicide watch. Paige gave up on him and no one could blame her. He was being eaten from the inside out. He didn't need anyone laying blame at his door. He quite capably managed that all by himself. The consequences of that downward spiral involved him doing some really stupid things, as if he was chasing death, begging it to take him too."

Charlie pressed a kiss against his fingers then pressed them to her cheek before letting go. "It must have been hard on all of you." She opened the can and drained the beans before dropping the pasta into one saucepan and the sauce ingredients into another.

"It was. Harder than you could imagine, especially when we'd lost Mom too. The attic and the garage itself held so many sad memories that seemed to outweigh the happy ones."

She stirred in a can of stewed tomatoes before turning to face him, her heart aching for the Calhoun family. "I'm so sorry."

He shrugged, the careless movement contradicting the tension in his spine. "It would have been easier to move away from Bigfork, but it wouldn't have mattered where we went, because the gossip would still have found us. Dad didn't want to leave Mom and Mitch behind. None of us did. We loved them too much to leave them. Dad said we should stay and let time heal our hearts and the minds of the people."

"Sometimes you can't stay. Sometimes you have to leave to see the truth." She turned back to the stove and dipped the spoon into the sauce. Scooping up a small amount, she blew on it to cool it before tasting.

He came to stand next her and dipped a spoon into the sauce to test it himself. "Oh, my God, that's good. Wait until I tell Mason what he missed out on."

Warmth flooded through her, the compliment a novelty she wasn't used to in a world where nothing she achieved was praised. "If there's any left over, I could save some for him?"

Chase squeezed her shoulder. "I think he'd like that."

Charlie let the smile forming on her lips grow. It seemed silly something as simple as a show of appreciation for a good pasta sauce should make her heart glow, but it did. She'd achieved. Taken a step forward. Grown.

She turned back to the sauce. "It's almost ready. Would you get the dinner plates out, please?"

Chase's arm dropped from around her and cooler, safer distance came between them. She could get too used to being cuddled into his side, too comfortable in his presence. And that would be dangerous. She hadn't come to Bigfork to find love. She'd embarked on this journey to find herself— Charlie Jackson, mother, artist, responsible and independent adult.

But there was no denying she liked the way Chase moved. The kitchen was small enough for him to brush against her as he reached for a drawer or cupboard door as he went through the motions of place setting. He moved with a fluid strength and sure steps, a strong man used to being in charge. In that way, he was a little like her father. In everything else, they were poles apart. Her father dominated and Chase ... mothered. A laugh bubbled in her chest and escaped through her lips.

Chase grinned. "What?"

She shook her head. "Just thinking. You're a good man, Chase Calhoun. Don't ever let the world change you." He frowned, and she lifted a hand to smooth the lines away. "Let's eat. Your family will be waiting for you."

A flicker of sadness showed in his incredibly blue eyes. Charlie wished she could make him happy again. She wished things could be different, that they'd met a long time ago. That he'd been the trigger to step off the cliff and start the journey to turn her life around. That she could be free to step up and kiss his inviting lips, soothe away his pain. But she had no business trying to fix others when she still had to fix herself.

Chapter Seven

CHASE ZIPPED UP his jacket, slipped on his gloves and beanie, and wrapped his scarf around his neck and mouth. Ahead, the pathway up the hill to the family cemetery loomed, low lights set into stone walls lighting the way. His father and brothers waited in silence, staring into the distance, alone with the sadness of their thoughts.

The lingering smell of the pines that stretched toward the mountains teased his senses as he drew in a deep breath through his nose. He wished it was still light enough to take comfort in the beauty of the ranch. Eight thousand acres of rolling fields and towering trees, the rustic charm of the main house with its pitched rooflines, natural wood, and stone walls. The warm, welcoming glow from the windows when it was lit up at night. And the sense of peace that surrounded them out here.

With all his heart he hoped this year would be different. That Mason's pain would be less, that the memories would have faded and the wounds would have healed just a little. For all of them.

"What took you so long?" Mason snapped out the words, the cold night air stealing them from his lips and turning his breath to vapor in the lamp light.

"Ease up, Mase. The boy's got to eat." Marty's hands trembled as he tried to get his gloves on.

"Cold as the devil's heart out here. Here, let me help you with that, Dad." Carter stepped forward and helped his dad with the gloves. "Let's get moving. We don't want to be out here too late."

"Stay at home then, Carter, if you're afraid of a little cold. I'll go on my own," Mason bit back.

Carter snorted. "You'll freeze your nuts off when you get lost."

Chase sighed as he recognized the snark in Mason's defense mechanism. One day his brother would stop hiding his hurt behind attitude. He ran forward and shoulder-bumped Mason who staggered under the unexpected weight and landed on his ass. "Race you to the top."

"You'd better run, asshole." Mason slapped damp fall leaves from his jeans as he stood.

Chase stole his beanie and ran, the thud of Mason's boots closing in behind him. At the top of the hill, Mason caught up, flinging himself on Chase's back and tackling him to the ground outside the gate to the family cemetery. They rolled around, throwing mock punches and trading insults, the way they had when they were boys. The only way Chase knew how to draw Mason out of his melancholy.

Beanie wrapped around his fingers, Mason stood and held out his hand. "Get up. Don't want to send you home to your new lady all wet and grubby. She might choose your younger brother instead."

Chase wanted to deny Charlie meant anything to him, but the words wouldn't leave his tongue. He'd only known her a few days, for God's sake. The thought of his brothers making a play for her shouldn't fill his heart with jealousy. He reached for his scarf which had come off during their scuffle before he accepted Mason's hand and got to his feet. Carter and their father caught up.

Marty put a hand on the gate and flicked open the wrought-iron latch. "Behave yourselves, boys. You don't want your mother to think I've raised a horde of hooligans."

Mason tugged down his beanie and shoved Chase, then stepped through the gate behind his father. Chase slapped him on the ass with a flick of his scarf before wrapping it back around his neck. Behind him, Carter chuckled, the sound drifting into silence as they reached the two grave-stones, side-by-side, one a little older than the other.

Familiar tightness clamped Chase's throat as he read his mother and baby brother's names engraved in the marble. Beside him, Mason shuddered and leaned closer. He hooked his arm loosely around his brother's shoulders. Marty knelt to light the candles, his hand steady for once, one for each family member. He added another two.

"We've got two new special guests at home tonight, Nora. You'd like young Charlie and Zoe, I think."

He continued to tell her of the things that had happened since they'd last visited, as if she could hear them. Chase embraced the sense of calm that descended on their small group. Perhaps she could hear them; perhaps the warmth that protected them from the cold came direct from her heart. His dad moved on to talk to Mitch. Mason stiffened beside him, the subtle shake in his shoulders warning Chase of the pain to come.

Dabbing at his eyes with the back of his glove, Marty stepped back. "Your turn, Mason."

Mason stepped forward and the grip on Chase's throat tightened painfully. He hated seeing his brother still broken after all this time. Mason said nothing. He knelt and touched the grass that covered the still slightly raised mound of dirt on Mitch's resting place. Head bent, he cried. Wracking, wrenching sobs that stabbed at Chase's chest and twisted his gut into knots.

Marty touched Mason's shoulder. "You've got to stop blaming yourself, Son."

Mason shook his head. "I can't, Dad. If it wasn't for me, Mitch wouldn't be lying here."

"It was an accident."

"No. I killed him. Because I was being an asshole that day."

"The piece about being an asshole is true, but you didn't kill Mitch." Carter stepped in beside him.

Mason shot him a death-stare. "Screw you, Carter."

Carter raised an eyebrow. "Want to take a shot at me? Will it make you feel better about yourself?" He sat beside him and presented his jaw. "Go on. Do it."

Mason ignored him. He pulled out a hip thermos from

his jacket instead. Chase sighed and sat down on the other side of Mason as his brother unscrewed the cap. They sat shoulder to shoulder, three brothers with their father standing behind them, and drank.

The bite of the whiskey eased the knot in his throat, relaxed the tension in his shoulders as Chase drank then passed the thermos back to Mason and their yearly ritual played out. But this time, it was different. The weight that normally settled on his shoulders at the sight of his mother's grave didn't come. The usual memories of that day that replayed in his mind stayed silent. In its place came a peace he'd never hoped to feel, as if his mother had finally managed to lift the guilt from his shoulders. And the only faces he saw in his mind were Charlie and Zoe's.

The whiskey warmed him, but the taste had changed. It no longer called to him to drink it, to drown the pain and guilt in its burn. A breeze swirled up around them in an otherwise still night, its breath warm instead of frosty. Then it was gone, sweeping away the orange and gold fall leaves, and drying the tears on his cheeks.

He hugged Mason closer as his brother drank, their heads close together. His own pain no longer sliced the way his brother's did. And the only thing that had changed for him was the arrival of a girl in town with no last name. He could almost hear the whisper of his mother's approval in the wind which made him wonder if he'd had more to drink than just a few sips. But no, the peace prevailed. If only it could touch Mason too. Perhaps his brother wasn't ready for it yet.

Mason drained the thermos and wiped his lips with the back of his hand. They sat a while longer in silence before Marty said a prayer and they snuffed out the candles. The bite in the cold night air returned.

"Come on, boys. Let's go home." Marty's voice echoed in the silence.

Chase and Carter stood, each taking an arm to help Mason to his feet. His brother had never been a big drinker, even less so since the accident. The whiskey would hit him hard and fast, aided by the dizzying cold that would meet them as they left the protection of the trees that surrounded the cemetery. In heavy silence, they descended the hill.

CHARLIE BLEW THE feathery strands of her bangs away from her face and tossed her sketch pad onto the sofa. She hadn't been able to settle since the door had closed behind Chase. Whatever state he returned home in, he deserved a friend. Especially after all he'd done for her and Zoe.

Unsettled, she crossed to the window to look out across the quiet ranch. The guests had retired to their cabins or heated tents. The low lights that dotted pathways and communal areas had been dimmed to a soft glow, and the first drops of rain kissed the glass in front of her face. A swirl of wind whipped up the needles shed by the larch trees that lined the west end of the property. Canada had opened its windows early this year to send arctic blasts Montana's way. She hoped the men wouldn't be out there much longer.

Charlie looked to the right up the gentle slope she'd watched Chase and his family take over an hour ago. Four tall figures, one only slightly hunched, made their way back down the slope, heads bent against the sting of the cold raindrops. She recognized Marty's rounder shape next to Carter. Chase and Mason walked side by side, arms around each other's shoulders. Who was carrying whom, she wondered.

As they drew closer, she realized Chase's steps were steady while Mason's dragged. She could almost feel the pain that shimmered around them. Mason, for all his blustery ways, seemed to be taking things harder than all of them. Charlie's thoughts drifted back to the pickup truck hidden out of sight at the very back of Calhoun Customs' showroom, draped in a cover to hide it from the world.

Charlie shivered and drew the long sleeves of her sweater down over her hands, clutching the edges in her fists before crossing her arms. Even though she wasn't close to her family in the way the Calhouns were, she couldn't imagine what it would be like to lose one of them or how she'd feel about it.

An idea flitted through her mind, taking shape, growing, building, excitement fizzing until she turned from the window and picked up her sketch pad. She'd known from the shape and size that under that cover was either an F250 or perhaps a Chevy Silverado. Her money was on the Silverado given the number of Chevys she'd counted in their fleet of pickups. A big canvas to work with.

Charlie flicked over the page she'd been working on to a fresh one and began to sketch the outlines, the picture forming in her mind as her pencil flew over the page. Blue flames on a black background, a gray skull in a brown cowboy hat emerging from checkered flags. The same theme would continue around the sides. Two skulls in a race, one ahead of the other, blue flames flaring out behind them. Colors ranging from light blue to navy until they merged with black. Even as she drew, her fingers itched to pick up the spray gun and make her design come to life on the pickup.

Would Chase come home tonight, or would he stay with Mason? The cabin felt empty and quiet without him. Her hand stilled on the sketch. She couldn't let herself get too used to having him around. He would be so easy to fall in love with. And falling in love with him would be a dangerous thing to do when she had no idea how long she could stay. She'd made a mistake once in her life and couldn't afford another. Not that she considered Zoe a mistake, but the relationship with her baby's father had been born out of rebellion rather than affection.

The cabin door opened, letting in a blast of cold air and the sound of raindrops falling heavily on the porch roof. Chase stepped inside, closed the door and dropped his boots on the mat before shrugging off his thick coat. He hung it on the peg by the door and blew on his hands before rubbing them together.

"You're still awake."

"I made a thermos of cocoa in case you needed something to warm you up."

He walked across the floor of the cabin, steady on his feet with no sign at all that he'd drunk too much. "Thanks."

Charlie moved her feet as he flopped down onto the sofa beside her, resting his head against the back of the sofa. With his eyes closed, she studied his face. Impossibly long, golden lashes brushed his skin, flushed with color as the heat of the cabin seeped in to warm him. That beautiful, kissable mouth drawn tight against the pain bottled up inside him. Her heart cried out to comfort him, to take him in her arms and soothe away the memories that drew his brow into a frown.

His eyes fluttered open and he turned his head toward her. Firelight flickered over his features, making him impossibly attractive in the glow. His eyes, as blue as the color she'd chosen in her mind for the design, searched hers. He seemed to hesitate, as if weighing up his words before he let them pass his lips. He didn't need to say them. She knew instinctively what he needed.

Closing the sketch pad, she dropped it on the floor along with her pencil. Then she held open her arms to him. Chase didn't hesitate. He stretched out beside her on the big, marshmallow cushions of the sofa, his head against her shoulder as she wrapped her arms around him and held him. Silence filled the cabin. Charlie stroked his hair and held him close, the rise and fall of his chest erratic against her side, the weight of his arm over her stomach as he held her right back.

She had no idea how to fix this broken man, but she could give him friendship and comfort.

His fingers stroked her hip through the warm flannel of her pajama bottoms. "I didn't get drunk."

"Is that a first?"

"Yes."

One word that said so much. Her heart ached for him. "That's good. It means you're healing."

"It's taken a long time."

"Some things take longer than others."

She continued to play with the short soft cut of the hair around his ear, her fingers brushing over the shell-shaped curve. She'd soothed Zoe this way so many times, but with Chase it felt nothing close to motherly.

He turned his face into her neck and tightened his hold, his breath warm on her skin, his lips cool as they touched the pulse that began to race there. She should stop him now, while she still had the strength to. He was hurting, and she knew better than anyone that being taken advantage of when a heart was broken never worked out well. But, darn it, he felt so good next to her, his body warm against hers, his lips soft against her skin in contrast to the scrape of his beard.

"Charlie?"

Her name whispered across her ear, as erotic as if his hands had touched her bare skin. She shivered against the flash of need that ripped through her. "Yes?"

"Stay with me tonight?" The lips that whispered the words trailed along her jaw, moved across the skin of her throat, delivering soft butterfly kisses wherever they touched.

Charlie swallowed and squeezed her eyes closed. If she stayed by his side, there'd be no doubting where this would lead, and it could jeopardize her journey to independence if it didn't work out. "I can't." Even though she wanted to.

He tugged her down gently until they were level. Vivid blue eyes, filled with sadness, searched her face for a moment before his head descended and his lips found hers. His kiss, soft and caring, had her melting into him with all the force of tender need. A light brush of the lips that searched while he sought permission to deepen it.

She reached up to touch his face, angled her body to align with his, and opened her mouth to his kiss. One kiss. What harm could it do?

His hand moved over her back, down across her hip, up over her arm to her shoulder. His lips moved in a sultry dance with hers, taking only as much as she'd give. And she wanted to give him more. A slight shift and she was in his arms, kissing him back, pressing into him with an urgency she'd never felt with anyone else, all the reasons she shouldn't be here with him this way fleeing from the heat of his touch. They were doing this for all the wrong reasons, yet it felt right. How could it be?

"Charlie." His breath shuddered out against her mouth as he shifted to move under her.

She fit into all his hard places as if her body was designed to do so. Every ridge, every curve melding with his, as if apart they were only pieces of the whole, but together they were a perfectly matched design.

His arms tightened around her even as his kiss softened, the heat seeping from it, leaving it warm and tender. He drew his mouth from hers, tucked her head into his neck, stroked her hair the way she had his, a lifetime and a kiss ago. Under her, his body was rigid, his desire evident, but he'd stopped. He needed comfort, not sex. She needed security not another one-night stand.

"I should go." She should retreat to the safety of her bedroom where her sleeping baby would remind her of the situation she was in, where the magic of Chase Calhoun couldn't reach in and compromise her plans for her future.

"I know." His actions belied his words as he dragged the throw blanket down off the back of the sofa and draped it over them. "Let me hold you for a while longer. You're warm and real, Charlie. And I need real. Just for a while."

Perhaps that was what she needed too. Any other man would have pushed on, pursued until she gave in. But not Chase. She snuggled into him, her arms relaxing to either side of him onto the sofa cushions as he rubbed circles on her back with the palm of his big, beautiful hands. Just for a while.

Chapter Eight

CHASE WOKE TO the soft glow of a lamp, the sound of rain on the cabin roof, and empty arms. He sat up to rub at the stiffness in his neck from sleeping with his head on the arm of the sofa. He missed the warmth and comfort of Charlie's curves against him. Somehow, she'd sneaked passed all his defenses.

She'd slotted right in, tackling tasks in the garage without being asked, helping when his dad's hands became unsteady or froze on the task, assisting Mason in between air brushing her design. As if she were born to it. A thought niggled at the back of his mind. Charlie was no stranger around cars. And then there was the fact that she no longer felt like a stranger.

The soft shuffle of feet made him look toward the kitchen. Charlie had Zoe up over her shoulder, soothing her with a gentle hand. His heart warmed. Whatever had brought her to his doorstep, no matter what she was running away from, he couldn't dispute the fact he was attracted to her. For the first time in forever, he'd come home from the grave sites and not felt the weight of guilt on his shoulders. Sadness, regret—yes. But not the all-consuming pain that had eaten at him in the past. If only Mason could find that same peace.

"You're awake." Her words were soft in the quiet cabin.

"Yeah. Everything okay with Zoe?" He stood and padded over to the kitchen.

"She's a little snuffly and warm, but her temperature isn't too high."

Chase rubbed a hand over Zoe's downy head. "She could be starting to teethe."

"That's what the book said too." She cuddled her baby tighter, two blonde heads close together.

A frown formed on his brow. Where were the baby's grandparents? Where was Charlie's mom? Surely she had family somewhere to support her? She shouldn't be needing to consult reference books for answers. He couldn't help her if he didn't know what it was she was running from. Chase leaned back against the kitchen counter and folded his arms.

"Charlie?"

She looked up at him over Zoe's head. "Yeah?"

"Honey, I know you're in some kind of trouble. Do you think you could trust me enough to help you?"

"It's not trouble on my tail, it's a journey to find the real me. The person I want to be, not the girl my family expects me to be. If I don't succeed, I'll always be under my father's thumb. But that's not to say he won't make trouble trying to stop me." Eyes as green as jade held his. "I can't thank you enough for how much you've done for me already."

"You're welcome to stay here as long as you want to. Dad is very pleased with your work."

Her gaze darted away. "I'd like that so much, but it's complicated."

"Only if you let it be."

"I'm scared, Chase. If I tell you the truth, you may not want me here at all."

"Have you committed a crime?" He couldn't imagine her doing something illegal.

She frowned. "I did a lot of irrational things out of anger that skirted the edges of the law."

"Since we're all awake, why not tell me what it is you think you've done wrong?"

Charlie shifted the baby onto her hip with a sigh. "I'm the rebel in the family."

"Not a crime the last time I checked. Every family has one. Grace is ours, but we still love her." That brought a smile to her face that made him want to touch her lips and trace the curve of her mouth.

"When you're a part of my family, there is no room for rebellion. You simply never cross the line my father draws. I crossed it many times." Sadness stole the smile from her eyes. She hugged her baby so close that Zoe uttered a muffled protest against her shoulder. "And now he wants to bring me back in line."

"You're a grown woman. Surely you can make your own choices?" He had no idea who her father was, but if he ever met him, Chase could think of a few things to say to the man.

She sighed. "I've made some very poor choices in life.

Some I'm not proud of and wish I could undo. The only choice I'm sure was the right one, is the choice I made to keep Zoe."

"Anyone can make a mistake, Charlie." He reached out to put a hand on her arm and draw her closer.

"But mine have the potential to harm people, and that includes my daughter."

"Then tell me, so we can work something out to fix it."

"I wasn't a nice person, Chase. It took falling pregnant with Zoe to make me realize that." She laughed, a bitter sound that tugged at his heart. "I was jealous of my brother's success and popularity, of him being allowed to follow his choice of career while I was designated to the background, forced to give up my dreams so I could 'support' my brother. My father is big on family support, but not in the same way yours is."

"What do you mean?" He folded his arms again because touching her when she appeared so vulnerable made him want to hold her again. He didn't think she was ready for that.

"Your father and brothers are warm with a real bond between you. My family is run more like a business corporation. We run to deadlines with every step carefully plotted and planned for maximum media effect. Affection is saved for when there is a media presence making it a necessary requirement to present ourselves as a normal, supportive family unit."

"Sounds awful." Chase couldn't imagine being part of a

family like that.

Mason might be a pain in the ass at times, Carter could be as stubborn as his black stallion, and the girls had been challenging during their teenage years, but he wouldn't change a thing when the moment they came home, the family would be whole again. Sure, there'd be arguments, but they'd be followed by hugs and forgiveness before everyone moved on from it.

"It is. To my parents, their marriage is a business partnership. My father is the celebrity CEO while my mother is the face of his charity dinners and social engagements. They're so cold and polite toward each other, it surprises me that they managed to procreate."

The bitter regret in her voice had him hauling her and Zoe into his arms, a complete package he had no will to resist. "If that didn't sound so awful and cold, I'd think you were making a joke, Charlie." He pressed a kiss to the softness of her hair then leaned back to take their weight against him, arms around her loosely, giving her the option to stay or go. He wanted her to stay. Badly.

"It's no joke. I rebelled against everything they stood for. I wanted to feel emotion, feel what it was like to be loved, appreciated, to be my own person rather than live in my brother's shadow. I did things to get that attention that I'm not proud of, but I won't ever regret that I gained Zoe out of that, even though there is a very real chance I could still lose her if my father continues to pursue the path of adoption."

Chase frowned and tipped her face, so he could read her

expressions. "I've seen you with Zoe, honey. There's no doubt you love that baby. Is that why you're hiding from him? Because he wants to have the baby adopted? Why?"

Her gaze searched his as she weighed up thoughts and words in her mind. He could see her thinking, hesitating. Could read the doubt in her eyes. It took ages for her to answer as a myriad of emotions flitted over her face.

He'd almost given up on an answer when she said, "Because I've tarnished the family name by my actions and now I've gone against his orders. I set out to prove to myself that I wasn't a rebellious brat, that I could be responsible and take ownership of my life and my baby. That I could change. It may not be enough. He's a powerful man with strong, influential connections and if he wants something done his way, he gets it."

Chase lifted his hands to her shoulders and set her back a little. "Just who are you, Charlie?"

She chewed her lip before dipping her head and staring at his chest, avoiding eye contact. He could feel the tension in her shoulders, the fear that shivered through her and realized she was putting everything on the line.

"My father owns TRJ Racing. My name is Charlotte Jackson."

CHARLIE WAITED.

"Charlotte Jackson." Her name rolled off his tongue.

She breathed in deeply, her eyes squeezed tight. If she couldn't see his face, she wouldn't see distaste mar his handsome face or his lips pull tight in disappointment. The way she was used to seeing every day growing up.

"Yes."

"Wow." His hands dropped from her shoulders to lodge on his hips. "Not what I was expecting. You look different without the dark hair and face paint."

"That was the disguise of an angry young woman. I'm not that girl anymore. This is the real me. Do you want me to leave?"

"What for?"

She drew on her courage to look him in the eye. "I lied to you."

"You withheld the truth. There's a difference. The way I see it, there's a reason you did. I'd like to know what it is."

"If I do go back, I know I'll be reliving the same nightmare. I won't have space to grow. My father will continue to make decisions for me. That includes adopting out my baby. And I've fought so hard against him doing that. I love my daughter with all my soul and I want to raise her. I don't want her raised by strangers." She drew in a breath and let it out again. "I don't want to go back to that life. I don't want to be Tony Jackson's rebel daughter, the troublemaker who makes his life hell. The sister portrayed by the press as the villain who puts the black mark on the Jackson name so that her brother's star can shine brighter."

"You're a total mystery to me, Charlotte Jackson. What

is it you've done that's so terrible?"

"Some really stupid things. Until I realized that no matter how hard I tried, my family was never going to see me, good or bad, so I made a promise to my baby that I would be the person I truly wanted to be. A good person. A good mom. And now I'm afraid that if he finds us, he'll make me go home and I'll lose everything before I've had a chance to achieve it."

He folded his arms across his chest. Arms she wanted to feel around her, holding her like they had last night, giving her courage and comfort.

Her arms ached from holding Zoe, a dead weight now that she'd gone to sleep on Charlie's shoulder. She should put her baby down, let her rest, but the thought of losing Zoe's comforting warmth made her hesitate. Zoe was exactly who she was fighting to keep.

Chase sighed and ran a hand through his already tousled hair. "No one should be afraid of taking control of their life."

"Fear is what made me grow up."

"Then if you've grown up, what happened in the past shouldn't matter."

"Tell that to the media and my parents. People have long memories, Chase."

Chase placed his hand on hers, tangling his fingers through hers and tugging her gently. "Why don't we sit where we can be more comfortable, and you can tell me? Zoe's no lightweight when she sleeps."

"She's growing so fast." How much longer could she do

this on her own? Raise a happy, healthy child when her father waited in the wings with the power to destroy everything she aimed to fix.

"You're doing just fine with her, Charlie. Don't doubt that. Stay true to what you're fighting for." He led her to the sofa, tugged her down beside him, and tossed the throw blanket across their legs. For a long moment, he studied her and Zoe, his features solemn in the firelight. "Our family knows a lot about gossip and blame. The blame comes mostly from within ourselves."

Charlie eased into the warmth against his side as he laid his arm around her and drew her closer. Zoe offered up a sleepy sigh. Charlie smoothed out her baby's frown with the tips of her fingers, her heart filled with love and pride for the tiny, little life she'd created. The only mistake she'd never regret.

"What made you come to Montana, Charlie?"

She looked up at Chase to find him watching her with a fire heating his look that warmed her all the way through. "I needed to get away from Florida. A complete change of scenery. A new start in life."

"A brave move on your own with a baby."

"Brave? My father would call it a dumb move."

"And running was the only option?"

Charlie thought a moment before answering, "Running, no. Hiding, yes, but only until I have a solid foundation under me to stand up to them. My family isn't like yours. We're not close in the way yours are. I'm the black sheep.

The one delegated to the shadows. My brother is the star, the go-getter, the favorite." The regret in her voice echoed in the space between them. "That's fact, not jealousy. I tried hard to make them see me, love me, but all they could see was Ronan and the commitments that swallowed their time and attention. It made me an angry teenager."

He shrugged. "You must have reason to feel that way."

"All my life I've lived in my brother's shadow. I wanted to go to art school, but it was considered a waste of money when my brother needed funding for his career. My father gave me a job in his marketing department. He said my 'talent' would be of better use in advertising rather than wasted on sketches and paintings. Apparently having a struggling artist in the family wasn't good for our standing in society."

"What gives him the right to make those decisions for you?"

Charlie grimaced. "My father is an old-fashioned tyrant. He wanted me to be a carbon copy of my mother, a perfectly groomed trophy wife with high-profile engagements. It just wasn't what I wanted."

"What do you want, Charlie?" He raised his free hand to touch her face, tangle a lock of her hair around his finger.

"I want to do what I'm doing for you. Designing, drawing, restoring. Giving things a second chance, breathing new life into them, giving them meaning. I want to love my job and what I do and provide a home for me and my daughter."

"What about Zoe's father?"

Her shoulders stiffened. She never wanted anything to do with that lying, cheating bastard ever again. He'd taken her father's money and run as fast as he could. "He's not in the picture. And he never will be. He made that perfectly clear."

"Sounds like a complete asshole."

"If only I'd been mature enough to see that through his charm and my rebelliousness."

Chase tugged gently on the lock twisted around his finger. "We've all made mistakes we wish we could go back and undo."

"I can't undo them, but I can make better choices for the future. I thought I could hide until I'd worked something out. A plan, a foundation to build on. But no matter how hard I try, I'll never be able to change my father's mind or his personality." Knowing she had to stand up against that eventually hurt too, but he'd had control for long enough.

"You can't change what people will think or how they'll react or what they'll try to do. It's what you plan to do that matters. It's about staying power. Deep inside you, you have that. You know it, or you wouldn't have taken this stand against your family. We'll have your back. You're here under our roof, and that makes you one of us."

She looked at him, her eyes taking in the promise that turned his eyes a deeper shade of blue, the perfect lips that hovered near hers, the heat she could feel transmitting through his knitted sweater.

It felt right that she should reach up her face to his. It felt right that his lips should touch hers as her eyes fluttered closed in expectation. And when she opened her lips to the gentle pressure of his mouth, it felt like heaven in his kiss.

INTOXICATING. HEADIER THAN the whiskey in Mason's thermos. Salty with tears. Sweet with comfort. Chase wanted to kiss her forever. Warm and inviting, her mouth was soft and pliant under his. Giving, taking, easing the pain from his heart, drawing hers to the surface so she'd share it with him.

More than anything else in the world, he wanted her to feel safe. If his mom were here, it would be exactly what she'd want him to do. Give another baby a chance in a place where so much heartache had dogged their steps.

He lifted his head mere inches from hers, not wanting to leave the welcoming, comforting space, but knowing he had to give her this opportunity to tell the truth without distraction or persuasion.

"Tell me the rest of your story, Charlie," he whispered into the space between them.

She sighed heavily and rested her head on his shoulder. "In my father's eyes, I was born a failure. First because I was a girl and second because I didn't want to race the circuit. From the time I could hold a pencil, I wanted to draw and create. Having an artist in the family didn't quite fit with their social standing, so they pushed me to do what they wanted for me. The harder they pushed, the more I rebelled."

Even as she said the words, her chin came out in defiance. Chase smiled. He liked a girl who could stand up for herself, but it would have come at a cost. "What did they want you to do?"

"Become a lawyer so I could run the team's legal department."

He winced even though he could totally imagine her in a fitted black business suit, rocking three-inch-heeled stilettos and a smile that would make his blood pressure rise. "Not your style?"

"Not even close. I went all out against it. The more criticism I attracted from my parents, the brighter my brother's star shone. 'Why can't you be more like Ronan, Charlotte? Why do you have to be so contrary?' He lapped it up, of course, taking every opportunity to throw it in my face as to who the favorite child in the family was."

"How did you feel about that?"

She shifted against him and he hugged her tight. "It hurt. The sharper the pain, the more I rebelled. There were parties that led to under-age drinking, protests leading to arrests, a fire at the sorority house I was in—all of it very bad publicity for the Jackson family."

Chase frowned. "Isn't that what all students do at some stage in their career?"

"Not when you're Tony and Leila Jackson's offspring."

The bitterness in her tone cut deep. "What happened then?"

"I got thrown out of Florida State University. My father buried me at the back desk in the team's marketing division where I couldn't possibly bring any more shame to the family."

"Still not terrible, criminal stuff, Charlie." He curled a lock of her hair around his finger and tugged. "You were just a brat."

"A fact my brother rubbed in my face very loudly and publicly at a team celebration party a little over a year ago. I was angry, humiliated, tired of constantly being talked down to, dictated to, and more than a little drunk."

Chase grimaced as his stomach took a nose dive. He had a feeling the fallout hadn't been pretty. "The final nail?"

"The very last one and sharper than any before it. I had no excuse other than blind fury fueled by too many cocktails and bottled up resentment."

"What did you do?"

"I left the party with a crew member who didn't have a healthy relationship with team management. He was one last warning away from being fired. A bad boy to the bone. On our way out, we passed my brother's Lamborghini on the driveway. Ricky dared me to do it and I was far enough gone not to have any good sense or functioning brain cells left." She shivered against him. Her breath hitched. "Ricky cut the fuel line and I dropped a match."

Chase bit down on the string of curses that lodged on his tongue. Shock had him stiffening his shoulders under her head. "You set fire to your brother's Lamborghini?"

She nodded. "Not my proudest moment. We didn't stick around to watch. The trouble is, I don't remember anything much after that. I know we kept drinking, but I woke up alone in a grubby motel room, only minutes before the sheriff arrived with a warrant for my arrest."

"Your father had you arrested?" The enormity of what she'd done stunned him, but that her own family would press charges against her rocked him to the core. What kind of a man would do that to his daughter?

"He said it would teach me a lesson."

"Did it, Charlie?"

She shook her head. "It only made me dislike them more when all I really wanted was for them to love me." Hot, wet tears soaked his sweater as she buried her face against him.

"What happened after that?"

Her words were muffled against the knit of his sweater, driven from her throat as she forced them out. "They released me on bail. Eventually the charges were dropped. It didn't matter. I was broken already. Then I found out I was pregnant with Zoe. From the start, they told me I had to give her up for adoption. At first, I agreed. I knew I'd come to the end of the line. That if I didn't change my ways, I'd only end up in worse trouble. But the first time I felt Zoe move, I knew ... I'd never be able to give her away."

"So, you told them you wanted to keep her?" He pulled his handkerchief out of the pocket of his jeans and handed it to her.

She slipped away from his side, blew her nose, dabbed at

her eyes and scrunched it up in the palm of her hand as she rubbed two fingers across Zoe's brow, relaxed in deep sleep. "Yes."

"And they said…"

"No, I had to give her away or they'd sign a declaration that stated I was an unfit mother. There was enough evidence and bad press to back up their threat."

This time Chase didn't hold back on the curses. Anger filtered through him.

"So, you ran away." Not a question, a statement. Had she had another option?

"I had no reason to stay. They were never going to love me. But I had a good reason to leave. In the months leading up to Zoe's birth, I had plenty of time to think, banished from the family home in Daytona Beach and imprisoned in my room at the house in the Hamptons."

Chase cocked an eyebrow and wondered if she was mocking herself or her parents' wealth. "A pretty impressive prison."

"It's only a house if there's no love to make it a home and give it life, Chase."

He had no argument with that, so he drew her and Zoe back to him and let her finish her story.

"I researched adoption, checked my rights. And when Zoe was born, I refused to give her up. My parents were away. Mom had a string of charity events to attend from Las Vegas to Singapore that kept her away for months. Dad was tied up on the circuit with races in full swing, so he sent his lawyer to deal with the adoption. I refused to sign the paperwork, which resulted in long-distance arguments and threats of what would happen if I didn't obey. So, I made a plan. I applied for jobs all over the country, got one, and planned a new life. I drew out my savings so I wouldn't have to use my credit card. It bought me time and distance until my car broke down and I had to rent a replacement. By that time, my father had his PI out looking for me."

"So, you kept moving, all the way across the country. Why stay in Bigfork?"

"Because everything I've been searching for is right here."

"What would that be, Charlotte?"

"A job I can be passionate about. Freedom, friendship, and a new start—a blank canvas on which to redesign my future."

He smiled, shifted closer and curled his fingers through hers where her hand rested on Zoe's blanket. "You have fire in your eyes when you say that. It's better than sadness and regret. Will you stay and fight for what you want?" He held his breath for her answer.

"Yes." She looked down at their joined hands, at Zoe, content in her arms.

"What happens when your father or his PI finds you? Is there enough here to make you stay?" He rested his cheek against her shoulder, lifted his face to hers, touched his lips to her skin. Her breath hitched as he trailed a path to her ear. "Is it just friendship we have, Charlie?"

She turned her face into the touch of his mouth. "I don't

know what it is we have yet," she whispered against his lips.

"We have all the time in the world to find out." He kissed her, slow and deep, exploring, searching, drawing, falling. Deeper and deeper.

Chapter Nine

CHARLIE ADDED THE finishing touches to the stallion's mane that flared out across the hood of Carter's newly finished pickup and tried not to daydream about kissing Chase last night. But, oh boy, could the man kiss. She touched a hand to her lips.

They'd talked. About her future, her plans, and the inevitable arrival of reality in town. With all her secrets out in the open, she could rebuild, prepared to continue the fight for her daughter. She still had so much to fix within herself before she could face her family.

A shadow fell over the hood, blurring the line she followed with her brush. Lifting it so she didn't smudge the paint, she looked up to find Marty watching her, hands on his hips, a slight tremor running through the muscles of his arms. She'd noticed the tremors had gotten worse since she'd arrived. How long before the disease stole his movement, his dignity?

"Looking good, girl. Carter's gotta be happy with that."

Charlie stepped back to admire her work, a stab of pride warming her blood. She'd put her heart and soul into this job, just as she had put everything into the new design she hoped would one day go on Mason's pickup. "You like it?"

"I darn well love it. You've got talent, girl."

She let the praise flow over her, inhaled it, embraced it. "Thank you, Marty."

The old man flicked an imaginary speck of dust off his sleeve. "You look so much like your mother. The way she was in the early days."

"I hadn't realized how much until you showed me the photograph. She's changed since then." When had the light gone from her eyes?

"She was a beauty. Crowned Miss Florida way back when she was just eighteen."

"Really?" Charlie raised her eyebrows. She hadn't known, had never seen any evidence of it either in trophies or photographs.

Marty leaned lightly on the fender and ran his hand over the smooth cream duco. "Your father snapped her up right out from under the noses of his rivals." He shook his head. "She changed after that. I guess she had to when your father made it big on the track."

"You were a big name too. I've seen photos of you on the podium."

Marty grinned. "First place to his third. He hated losing. Especially to me."

"Why is that?"

He winked. "Because I had more skill than he did, but he had old money behind him."

That sounded exactly like her father. He believed he

could buy everything. Including people and happiness. "Do you miss it, the rush, the adrenaline, the win?"

"No." Sadness clouded his eyes. "I had a wife I hardly ever saw, children who grew up with only glimpses of me. I had a short time to enjoy them all before I had to leave again. No time at all to make a real home for them. Instead they lived in the attic above the shop while I raced cars to make money to build my dream. This." He pressed his shaking hands into the pockets of his coveralls and looked around the garage. "And then it was too late. She was gone, and I had six kids to raise alone. I'd give back every trophy I won just to have that time over with her and do things differently."

Tears stung her eyes at the heartbreak in his. "I'm sorry."

"Don't be. What I'm telling you, girl, is to follow your heart and trust that it will lead you where you need to be. Sometimes we let our head stand in the way of happiness."

"What if I don't know what my heart wants?" Movement to her right caught her eye and she looked up to see Chase in the doorway to his office, Zoe in his arms, wide awake and making happy baby noises up at him.

"Oh, I think you know exactly what your heart wants, young lady." He tapped the fender with his palm and chuckled. "All you need to do is reach out and take it."

Charlie tore her eyes away from Chase and met Marty's smiling eyes. "Oh no. No. Don't go getting ideas now. I'm here to do a job. That's all."

"You had the job in the bag the moment I laid eyes on

those designs. You're exactly who we need here at Calhoun Customs. And I think you're exactly who my son needs too. But I'll let you make up your own mind about that."

"It's complicated."

"Isn't everything in life?"

Marty pushed away from the pickup as Chase wandered over to stand next to him. Marty reached out to tickle Zoe's cheek with his forefinger and was rewarded with a gurgle. Zoe waved a fist around, almost as unsteady as Marty's, and tried to catch his hand. Charlie's heart squeezed around the moment. Her father would never engage with Zoe the way Marty did, even if he was given the chance to. And her mother's heart was too frozen to show real love.

Marty's words from earlier flitted through her mind. What had made her mother change when she'd met her father? What was she like before she was crowned Miss Florida? What dreams had she sacrificed to become Tony Jackson's wife? The paintbrush slipped from Charlie's fingers, leaving a blob of brown paint where it shouldn't be. Quickly, she reached for her rag to wipe it cleanly away. That was all in the past now, she had to focus on what was to come. Her future. Zoe's future.

"Everything okay, Charlie?"

Chase's words, soft and warm, reached her ears. The same soft, warm voice that had comforted her last night. The man with the hard arms, firm chest, and strong heart that had drummed out a soothing rhythm beneath her ear until she'd fallen asleep in his safety zone. To wake in the morning, wrapped around him on the sofa, a blanket covering them and her baby safely asleep in the porta-crib beside them. Men like Chase were too hard to find, too easy to love, and too special to taint with the tar of her brush. What if she hadn't changed enough?

This morning, driving into town, seeing the smile on his face, the quick glances he kept sending her way, all of it had her tied in knots. Not that anything had happened on the sofa, except for a few sizzling hot kisses then he'd held her while they slept. But, God, she wouldn't mind waking up to that every morning with his lips brushing her hair and cheek with a gentle "good morning". It was the most treasured she'd felt in forever.

"Charlie?"

"Hmm?" She looked up and caught his twinkling blue eyes focused on her and a blush crept into her cheeks.

"I asked if everything is okay?"

"Oh…" The sound came out more like a breathless sigh.

She caught it and cleared her throat at the same time as Marty delivered a soft, knowing chuckle. Charlie shot a warning look his way but couldn't maintain the heat in it when his laugh was so infectious.

"Everything is just fine. All good." She stuffed the rag back into her pocket and held out her arms for her daughter. "I'll go and feed Zoe while the paint dries. Then we can apply the clear coat and bake her, and she's all done. The pickup, I mean. Bake the pickup."

Marty laughed harder. Chase frowned. Oh, dear God,

his father was right. All this talk about following her heart. She'd found what her heart wanted more than her parents' approval, and she was in no position to claim it. Not until she could face her father and the sting of his reprisal with her head held high and proof beyond doubt that she could take care of herself and her baby.

CHASE SHOVED HIS hands into his pockets and rubbed them against the rough denim. If he hadn't, he would have hauled Charlie back and kissed her senseless. His eyes were still gritty from lack of sleep because he hadn't been able to close them while she'd lain wrapped around him, breathing softly into his neck. Inhale. Exhale. Soft breaths that raised his temperature and tore at his heart at the same time. One step away from falling and tumbling headfirst into everything Charlie.

He wanted to wring her father's neck. Shake her mother out of her ice castle. And ram his fist down her brother's throat for being such an *asshole*. His Google search had turned up all the media articles she'd told him about, including the one showing the charred remains of her brother's Lamborghini. From the comments he'd made to the press, Chase reckoned the pretentious little asshole had got what he'd deserved. Who threw their little sister under the bus like that?

The unmistakable roar of anger ripped through the

doorway from the showroom into the garage, followed by sound of something hard slamming into metal. Marty looked up, his eyes meeting Chase's, with a helpless shake of his head.

"I'll handle it, Dad. Stay here, okay? Keep Charlie and Zoe away."

Marty nodded. Chase took long, steady strides into the showroom. The tarp had been ripped from Mason's battered pickup and lay in an angry, discarded bundle on the carpeted floor. Mason swung the sledgehammer, high on bitter anger, muscles quivering under the weight of each impact. His blow landed on the already battered hood, the metal shuddering under the contact. Every year it was the same. Every year the battered pickup took another beating until it no longer mattered which scar had come from the accident and which one had been self-inflicted. With every strike of the sledgehammer, his brother lost another piece of his soul.

Outside the big windows, rain drifted down at the command of the fall weather gods, the ice-cold drops touching the faces of a group of curious onlookers. Chase stayed back out of the range of flying shrapnel and activated the remote that would bring the blinds rolling down the windows to shut out the view from the street. Molly would see his signal over at the Old Time Five and Dime, warm up some of Mason's favorite scones, whip up some cocoa in takeaway cups and be ready to come over as soon as the danger had passed.

"That's enough, Mason." Chase let his voice drift into

the silence that followed the next blow.

"It's. Never. Enough." Mason punctuated each word with the crash of his fist on the battered roof of the pickup. "Never."

"It's been five years. It's time to let go."

His brother turned on him, eyes wild with anger and guilt. "Tell that to all those people out there who give me the stink eye at the same time every year. Tell that to the boy who lies up there on the hill in a cold damn grave."

"That's because *this* is here to remind them. To remind us. And you." Chase stepped up to take the sledgehammer from Mason's hand, limp now that all his power was spent. "Hiding it under a tarp won't change anything. We fix it, or we scrap it. Today's the day you choose." He said that every year, and every year they dragged the tarp back over it to hide its multitude of sins. Every year as they did so, he hoped that next year the outcome would be different.

"I can't." Mason dropped his head in his hands, his shoulders.

"You should." Chase dragged him into a hug, used to the resistance he put up.

Mason let his big brother hold him for a short while before he shoved him away, hard. At the back of the room, Charlie stood frozen. Where the hell was Zoe and why hadn't she stayed out of the way like he'd instructed? She took careful steps toward them, clutching her sketch pad to her chest, her face pale under the spotlights in the showroom. Chase shook his head, willed her to back off, but she set a defiant tilt to her chin and kept walking. Damn it. Now wasn't the time for her to exercise her stubborn streak.

She reached them and placed a hand on Mason's sleeve. Chase held his breath. Mason in this mood was volatile, a volcano of emotion ready to bubble over and burn anything and anyone in his path. But instead of going psycho on her, he dropped his gaze to the pale fingers with their neatly shaped nails, turning his clenched fist up as he followed the line of her arm until his eyes reached her face. The tension eased from his shoulders and his fist released, baring his palm for Chase to see the damage he'd done to his hand.

"Mason, I have something to show you," she whispered into the tense silence, her voice hesitant, wary.

"Honey, this isn't a good time …" Chase hated that at any moment Mason could snap and take his bad mood out on Charlie.

"Shut up, Mother," Mason growled. "What is it, princess?"

Charlie clutched the sketch pad tighter to her chest. Doubts flickered across her beautiful face. Chase wanted to reach out and drag her away from the monster that taunted them with its damaged body and steadfast silence. She chewed her lip and a monster of a different kind rose in him as he noticed Mason's gaze follow the movement.

"I had an idea for a design come to me last night, so I drew it for you."

Mason frowned. "Why?" He barked out the word, but she didn't shrink from it.

"Because I think it might be exactly what you want. I think it might even be what Mitch would have liked."

"Don't mess with me, princess." His growl turned to a snarl. "You didn't even know my brother."

"Mason." Chase gripped Mason's shoulder and drew him back out of Charlie's face.

She tipped her stubborn chin up a little higher and turned her sketch pad around for them to see. "This is the design for the hood. The skulls represent races won and lost, the flag means it's over, but not for long. Only until the next race. And the cowboy hats ... well, this is Montana after all."

Mason's sharply indrawn breath had Chase wanting to see what she'd done, but he could wait. Tension drained from Mason's muscles, the danger of his anger past.

Charlie flipped the page. "And this is for the sides. Look at it, Mason. Really *look* at it." She pressed the sketch pad into his hands.

He looked, holding the page between his thumb and forefinger, poised to tear it out. He didn't. Instead he listened to Charlie in a way Chase had never seen Mason listen before.

A little smile spread across her face, signaling her victory. "Your two skulls again, one regenerating, the other staying the same. Chasing each other across the sky, together yet apart, the blue flame that binds them together burning eternal. Mitch will always be with you, Mason."

The burn of loss lodged in Chase's throat. He hoped Mason would see exactly what she'd drawn and how perfect it was for the pickup. It might even spur him on to fix it or, at the very least, not continue to destroy it or himself further.

When Mason spoke, his voice was tight. "Do you seriously think showing me a pretty picture will make things right?"

"No, nothing will make what happened right. We can't undo the past, but we can make amends. We can make things brighter again. Do you think Mitch would want you to stay angry at a chunk of metal? Do you expect the people, standing outside that window watching you, to forgive you when you can't forgive yourself?" She stepped into Mason's space and Chase held his breath. "Do you think your mom would want this for any of you?"

Mason's head jerked up and he considered her with narrowed eyes and a bitter twist to his mouth. "So now you know what my mother thinks too, princess?"

"I know I wouldn't want to see a child of mine unable to forgive himself for an accident."

"It wasn't an accident."

"It was. You didn't make it rain that day. You didn't set out to make the road slippery."

"I was showing off." He shouted the words at her, but she didn't flinch.

Chase stepped forward. She glared at him, so he stepped back again. "You made an error in judgment and you paid the price. You can't bring Mitch back by beating the shit out of a piece of metal, Mason. But you can honor him by making that pickup beautiful again, by paying tribute to his memory, by showing those people out there that you're ready to forgive yourself. If you do, they will too."

The fight leeched out of him. "How do you know so much, princess?"

"Because I made an error in judgment too."

"What did you do?"

"I set fire to my brother's Lamborghini."

"You … *Why*?" Mason's features screwed up into a mask of confusion.

"Because he was being a nasty little shit and I was done taking it. He's nowhere near as nice and deserving of forgiveness as you are."

Mason thought on it a minute. "You've got balls." Reluctant admiration colored his tone as he turned away and shoved the sketch pad into Chase's hands, shoulders hunched around his thoughts. "Here. You look at it. I need a drink. I smell Molly's cocoa. And, Pyro?"

"That's my name now? No more 'princess'?"

"*Pyro*, if you want to paint it, you need to help fix it."

The half-smile his brother offered, less mocking than usual, brought hope to Chase's mind that, at last, his brother might be healing. Victory had the sweetest taste. Sweeter than the marshmallows in Molly's cocoa, which had to be the best tasting stuff he'd ever had. His brother walked away, solemn but no longer bone-deep angry. Chase's fingers traced the lines of Charlie's sketch. She'd brought a small smile to Mason's lips and perhaps a little peace to his heart. It made him fall a little harder for the girl he'd found sleeping among the shattered memories of their lives.

Chapter Ten

BACK IN THE garage, with Zoe and Mason settled, Charlie's phone vibrated as a message came in. She'd charged it and turned it on for the first time since leaving the Hamptons. A myriad of emails, missed calls, messages, and angry texts from her family had greeted her. She'd deleted them all without reading them.

She pulled the phone from her pocket and dialed into her voice mail to hear the cold, hard tones Tony Jackson saved for his most disobedient employee.

"Charlotte. This is your final caution. You have shamed this family enough. We have the adoptive parents of the child waiting to hear from you. Yet again, you have bridges to mend. One more week is all you have. I will not tolerate this behavior any longer."

The *child*. As if her baby was a spare part he'd ordered and not received rather than a sweet child who deserved to be loved and cuddled like the precious gift she was. Anger shifted to a stab of regret as her thoughts turned to the people who'd come forward to adopt her. She hadn't meant to hurt them. Her heart ached for them, but there would be other babies needing homes. Others more in need of a stable, loving family than Zoe. Zoe had a mother who loved her and people around her who cared. So much more than they'd have if she obeyed her father's demands.

One week wasn't long enough to stop the mighty Tony Jackson from exercising his influence over the law and tearing her reputation as a capable parent to shreds. It didn't matter to him that his wayward daughter had mended her ways and grown up, taking responsibility and motherhood seriously. All that mattered was he had full control over the perfect image of family he'd created when he had no real idea of the kind of fabric that weaved a real family.

Chase touched her shoulder lightly. "Everything okay?"

She wanted to say yes, but the word hitched on a hard-drawn breath. Things between her and Chase had changed since she'd spent the night in his arms. A subtle shift from friendship to something more. Something so much more dangerous because she couldn't let herself be drawn into the wonder of it, the promise of a future and a happy-ever-after.

She'd known him less than a week, yet it felt like she'd known him forever. She'd fallen in love with Marty, the kind of grandfather her baby deserved to have. Fallen for Carter and Mason because they were the kind of brothers she'd always wanted. Fallen for Chase in a way she'd never thought possible. Hard and fast, like a driver sneaking into the slipstream, blindsiding her to take the flag, stealing her breath, the adrenaline and her win.

"Charlie?"

She'd been so strong and brave until now. Until the look

of concern on his face stole her heart and bravado in one smooth move of his lips. Her throat closed tighter around the fear that robbed her of words. She hadn't done enough yet to keep Zoe with her. She hadn't had enough time to prepare to take a stand against her father again, not face-to-face. She still had so much more to do to establish her foundations in this new life she'd chosen.

Chase cupped her face, his palms warm, stealing some of the chill from her skin. "Bad news?"

She focused on those deep blue eyes, the care in them, the solid reassurance and strength in his presence. "Kinda. That was a message from my father." Her lips pulled tight. "Well, more of a warning really."

He dropped his hands from her face and curled his fingers around hers. "Come into the office and we'll deal with it." He tugged her inside.

"I'm not sure you can help. I'm out of time and I've asked so much of you already." He stayed close, his hands on hers, the cell phone a brick between them, a reminder of what she had yet to face.

"Tell me what's going on. The least I can do is help you come up with a plan."

"My father doesn't care about any plans. The only thing he cares about is image and reputation and making sure everyone obeys his iron will."

"What did he say to you?"

Charlie drew in a deep breath and let it out on a steady sigh. "He's given me a week to change my mind on the adoption."

"And then?"

"He's coming for us. With my phone turned on, he'll have had Ed pinpoint my location."

"Then we need a plan."

"He has enough cause to fight this. Enough people power on his side to follow through with his threat to have me declared an unfit parent. Damn it, Chase, he won't care that I've changed or that I'm trying to make a new start on my own." She hated the bitter taste on her tongue. She had to find a way around this fast. "I can't be what he wants me to be. The perfect daughter, the trophy on his shelf."

"You're so much more than that, Charlie." He wrapped his arms around her and pulled her in for a hug.

Charlie let herself relax against him, absorb the heat and solid strength, her arms slipping around his waist to hug him back. She wanted to let him take control, fix this, make the problem go away. But if she did, she'd just be letting another man control her bid for independence.

"He won't give up. My father doesn't like to lose. But I can't let him take my baby. She's mine. Zoe is what made me take a good long, hard look at the path I was on. Without her, I know I'll be right back there again, spiraling into self-destruction."

"We'll fight it together, honey. You'll have the Calhoun clan right behind you."

"He'll use your support for me against you. It will touch everything your family has worked so hard to achieve. There is nothing he will stop at to get what he wants, and that could destroy your reputation and your business." She pressed her face into his shirt, inhaled the spicy scent of man, cologne and reality. "I can't let him destroy you too. It'll be better if I take Zoe and move on."

"And if you do that, you'll leave Carter with an unfinished paint job, steal Molly's joy ..." He turned her around, so she could see out the office window where Molly's smile was wide as she played with Zoe, happiness radiating from her as she made cheerful, cooing noises Zoe copied. Then his fingers touched her chin and drew her attention back to his face, and the blue eyes she could lose herself in. "You're no quitter. Let me help you, Charlie. I can't fight your battles for you, but I want you to know that you'll have backup every step of the way."

Confidence seeped back in to warm her. He understood she'd never be free until she stood up for herself and faced the monsters that had shaped her life. "I know my rights. He has no authority to adopt Zoe out without my permission."

He smoothed the bangs from her forehead. "Then that's where we'll start. How long do we have?"

"A week."

"Tight, but not impossible."

"What if he comes after you and your family?"

A smile spread across his face, reaching his eyes and making the corners crinkle. "We happen to like a good fight. My father's competed against yours before and won. It'll give Dad something to look forward to."

Unease skittered along her skin. "This isn't a pissing contest, Chase. It's my child's future."

Dismay stole his smile. "Oh, honey, I'm sorry. I don't mean it that way at all. Dad had to fight to keep his six children, especially Trinity being a newborn. He knows loss more intimately than any of us. Knows what it's like to lose a child. And a wife. You and Zoe have crept into our hearts, Charlotte Jackson, and we won't want to lose either of you any time soon."

She wanted to cling to the promise in his eyes and the hope in her heart, but the nagging voice of reason insisted on placing doubt in her mind.

CHASE RUBBED THE tiredness from his eyes as the words on the screen of his laptop blurred in front of him. He looked at Charlie where she sat next to the fire, Zoe asleep in her arms.

The trip home from the garage earlier had been in silence. They'd cooked and eaten a meal without many words passing between them and while he'd searched the adoption agency rules for loopholes her father might try to wiggle through, she'd held on tight to everything she cared for in the world.

"Have you had contact with the baby's father, Charlie? Has he given consent to adoption?"

With a sigh, she turned sad eyes to meet his. "Ricky signed an affidavit declaring he'd make no claims on Zoe. He was happy to take his two-hundred-thousand-dollar payoff and leave without a criminal charge against him."

"Your father paid him off?" Chase disliked Tony Jackson more and more. He'd like to teach the man a lesson he'd never forget.

A sad smile twisted her lips. "Ricky was a player. The money would have been too good to refuse. He was never going to be in it for the long haul anyway. I made a mistake that night and I'm not proud of it. I was fired up by alcohol, rejection, and rebellion."

"So, the only avenue your father has is to go the unfit parent route." He couldn't imagine a father doing that to his daughter. Would it matter at all that she was turning her life around? If the rumors were true, Tony Jackson's heart was an unbreakable stone wall.

"In the months before Zoe was born, they never visited me or called. My marketing portfolio was taken away from me and I was placed on unpaid personal leave. I had a lot of time to think. They weren't there to witness how feeling Zoe move, knowing I was growing a life inside my belly, made me change. I doubt it would have made a difference to their thinking even if they had."

"They abandoned you."

"No, they punished me." A deep sigh left her throat. "But I was used to the silence. I preferred it to seeing the disappointment in their eyes that I'd failed to meet their expectations and requirements. I needed that time to find myself, see what I'd become. They did me a favor, except the outcome wasn't what they wanted. They wanted me to become like them—ambitious, driven, cold robots not afraid to trample on anyone who got in the way of their success."

"Why was your father so determined to have Zoe adopted out?"

"Because she would be a blemish on the family's reputation, a constant reminder that their daughter had tainted their perfect family portrait and a lure for the media to keep regurgitating my mistakes to throw in their face with every victory my brother scored on the track."

Chase felt each stab of her words. He couldn't comprehend how cold and hard her family sounded. So different from his own father who had fought so hard to keep his children. A man they respected and adored. The man who would need his children now more than ever as his health declined. And they'd give him everything they could in return for never giving up on them, no matter how bad things got.

A solution to her problem simmered in his mind and took shape. The more he thought about it, the more the idea grew on him. He set aside his laptop, stood to walk across to where she sat, and knelt in front of her. In the firelight, her pale skin was smooth. Like polished marble and just as cold when he lifted a finger to stop the tear tracking down her cheek. Her eyelashes fluttered down to conceal the hurt in her eyes.

"Charlie, honey, look at me." He cupped her face between his hands, rubbed his thumbs across her cheeks. Her eyes opened, and she looked at him, the sadness in them making a lump form in his throat. "I think I may have a solution."

"Does it involve a good lawyer?"

He hated the desperate hope in her question, knew he'd do anything to help her. Had known that very first day he'd met her in Molly's store that this girl would be special, that she could be the one to make him whole. He'd lost his heart piece by piece when he hadn't been looking for anyone to lose it to.

"It involves a minister."

A frown formed on her brow, her eyes searching his. "A minister?"

Her emotions floundered from confusion to comprehension, flitting across her features. Her mouth formed an 'oh' and his stomach did a nerve-filled back flip. "Marry me, Charlie."

"Chase …"

"It would make perfect sense. Together we have more power than you do alone. We can show them how you've fitted in with the community, with the family. They'll see you have a job and a home and a family to support you. A real family. A father for Zoe and a secure future."

"That's a big leap, a huge commitment." Disbelief strangled her words. "You'd do that for me? I'm a stranger. A messed up, high-risk stranger you met less than a week ago."

"You've slept in my guest room, on my sofa, in my arms. You stopped being a stranger the day I brought you tea and a muffin under that tree near the dock."

"It's a beautiful, generous offer, Chase. But my father would see right through it for what it is. He'd know we're faking it and all it would do is give him more ammunition to fire his gun."

"What if we weren't faking it? You can't deny there is chemistry between us. We can make it work." He let the words whisper between them, afraid that if he said them too loud, they'd shatter and break.

"And what happens when that chemistry is spent, and the fire burns out? The old Charlotte lived that way, the new one can't afford to. I can't let Zoe become collateral damage in a relationship born out of the wrong reasons." She leaned forward and pressed her lips to his in a far too brief and fleeting kiss. "You're a wonderful, generous, kindhearted soul with a mothering complex that makes you care too much. You're a rare find, Chase Calhoun, and you make me very afraid."

He held her face to his, not ready to let her go. He drew in a breath of the essence of Charlie. "You have nothing to be afraid of with me."

"I'm afraid of falling in love with you. That if I do, I might break you. There is enough of the old Charlotte in me to do that, and it scares me."

"I'm willing to take the risk," he whispered against lips that still held the taste of hot cocoa and honey.

"And I won't use you that way when you've done so much for us." She pulled away, leaving nothing but cold air between them. "I have to find my own feet for this fight, but it helps knowing that I have your support. I've still got a lot of growing to do and part of that journey involves standing up to my father in a way that isn't meant to antagonize him."

Chase sat back on his haunches with a sigh. "Then we need a plan." He pushed up to his feet and walked back to his chair, picking up his laptop again. "One that involves a doctor, a lawyer, and a few favors to be called in, and I know exactly who to call."

She smiled at him from across the room and despite her rejection of his offer, she wasn't unmoved by what flared between them.

Chapter Eleven

CHARLIE PUSHED DOWN the feeling that something bad was about to happen and dragged the cover off Mason's battered pickup. She rolled it into a ball as she assessed the damage. Very little of the bodywork had escaped unscathed, either from the accident or Mason's attempts with the sledgehammer. She'd seen accident damage before, knew the work that went into fixing it, if it could be fixed at all. The hood had suffered most of Mason's frustrations, the passenger side of the cab bore the imprint of a tree trunk, the roof panel was battered from the rollover and the sides of the cargo bed resembled a crushed aluminum can. Mason might have been better off buying a brand-new truck.

She grimaced at the thought that the truck bore an accurate resemblance to the tatters of her life. She wore almost as many scars as the mangled wreck in front of her. Out the corner of her eye, she saw Mason enter the garage, take one look at his pickup, and head back out the door again. Disappointment flooded her. This had been his suggestion after all. But perhaps, like her, he wasn't quite ready to face his nemesis yet.

Marty stepped up beside her. "What do you think, Charlie girl?" He ran a hand along the battered side as if he were trying to erase the damage with a simple touch. "Do you think we can rebuild her?"

Charlie couldn't begin to imagine what was in his thoughts as he faced the monster that had stolen his youngest son. "I'd like to try, but I'm afraid it might not be the right thing to do. Giving it new life won't erase the bad memories for any of you." Marty's fingers trembled against the scarred paintwork, and Charlie wondered if it was Parkinson's or the weight of the memories that made them unsteady.

"When does a ghoul become a ghost before it becomes a memory?" He peered into the cargo bed, lost in thought for a moment. "My boys have been haunted for long enough. They've been existing, not living. Mason for the last five years. Chase for too many years before that. I think I relied on him too much being the eldest. Nora wouldn't want this for them. The sadness, the unhappy memories."

Charlie picked up a screwdriver. Prying off the cover on the tailgate lock, she put her weight behind the tool to loosen the screws that held it in. "I think you're right." She removed the screws and jiggled them around in her palm, running her thumb across the thread. "Do you know, when I was up in the attic, I got this really safe, comfortable feeling. Like an embrace, a warm hug, as if she was still up there, watching over everyone. Sounds fanciful, doesn't it?"

Marty turned to drag an empty cardboard carton closer for her to toss the parts into. "It sounds exactly like Nora. She loved to hug the children. Every day. Even though they were a boisterous bunch and always up to some kind of mischief." He smiled softly. "She would have liked you, Charlie. She would have liked the change you've brought to Chase. He smiles more, talks more, walks taller."

She wanted to say she'd noticed, but it was better his father didn't know how much she liked to watch Chase walk, the sway of his hips and width of his shoulders, the strength in his spine and the muscles on his back. How he'd felt under her when she'd slept at his side on the cramped confines of his marshmallow sofa. How much she really wanted to say yes to his proposal.

"She would be proud of the job you've done raising him. You helped him grow into a responsible adult with a conscience. He's a rare breed, Marty." And because thinking of him made her want to seek him out, to absorb everything he encompassed, feel his arms around her again, she focused on the cold steel under her hands instead. "Pop those clips on the bed liner, would you? Once I get the tailgate off, we'll drag it out and see what's under it." She picked up a punch and a mallet, hesitating as Marty continued to stare into the empty shell of the cargo bed. "Are you sure you're okay with this?"

"Yeah. I will be. Didn't move it in here for nothing. Talk me through it, girl. Has Chase talked to the lawyer yet?"

She looked over at the office as Chase appeared in the doorway. "This morning. And I have an appointment with Doctor Ponti for an assessment on Thursday that will include blood, alcohol, and drug testing for her health report."

"I think it's ridiculous that you have to jump through hoops to prove anything to your father," Marty grumbled.

"It's preparation more than proof. I want to be able to field anything he throws at me." Chase headed to the back of the garage and hesitated in the alcove at the base of the attic stairs. She nodded in his direction and aimed her question at his father. "Is Chase okay?"

Marty followed her gaze. "Ah." He frowned. "It still catches him unawares sometimes. The memories of what happened to Nora. Catches me too. It's why we moved out to the ranch. Took a long time and the help of friends to strip out the home we'd made upstairs and turn it into storage. It was the best move for all of us. What Nora would have wanted."

Chase gripped the railing hard, squared his shoulders, and raised his head. Charlie placed the punch and mallet on the lowered tailgate of the pickup. She remembered the day the sunlight reflected off the window, how she'd felt drawn to the attic, led by an invisible tug that had drawn her up those stairs, leaving uncertainty and disquiet behind. Nora wouldn't want Chase to be afraid either. "I'll be right back, Marty."

A slow smile spread across his face. "Sure thing. Take all the time you need."

She pressed a kiss to his cheek and patted his shoulder. "Thanks." Then she made her way across the garage to Chase.

He stood with one booted foot planted on the first metal stair, his hand gripping the railing, knuckles white, gaze pinned to the top landing, mouth drawn in a tight line. She stopped next to him inside his line of vision.

"Need me to go up and get something for you?"

He shook his head, his eyes staying glued on his destination. "Last time I went up there a sandwich and a can of beans short and I came down with a girl and a baby. I hope there aren't any more surprises up there."

"Hmm, I see your point." She crossed her arms and leaned on the railing. "If you're afraid, I can go up ahead. Fight off a few rabid dust bunnies, hack a path through the metal shelving." She slipped in under his arm to face him and trailed a finger down his shirt buttons. "Dust off the old Charger back seat. So, you can ... you know ..." She shrugged one shoulder and drew his gaze to hers. "Take a seat. An old man like you would get puffed out climbing those stairs."

The hand not gripping the railing like a lifeline came around to anchor her against him. "You sure know how to distract a guy, Charlie. And does this feel like an old man's body to you?" He hauled her closer against every defined ridge.

She ran her hands up the front of his shirt, across his shoulders, and down his arms. "A pretty fit old guy." She pried his fingers loose from the railing. "Let me hold your hand in case you fall, Grandad," she teased.

"Grandad?" His eyebrows shot up making his forehead

wrinkle. "You're pushing your luck. There's like ... what? Five or six years between us?"

"Six years and a metal step." Charlie took a step backward up the stairs which brought her almost eye level with his bewitchingly blue eyes. "What are we looking for up there?"

"Paperwork from the time my grandparents set the authorities on Dad to try and have us taken away from him. I thought it might prove helpful in your case as research." His grimace said everything about the painful memories that would be released when he opened that box on the past.

She stopped, her hand on his chest, his heart beating under her palm, her teasing mood evaporating. She'd seen his struggle and come over to distract him, help him the way he was helping her, to face whatever stopped his progress into the past. "You'd do that for me?"

Chase nodded. "I know what it would have done to us as a family if we'd been split up. I don't want that to happen to you, Charlie. We grew up without a mom. As much as we love Dad, and Molly stepped in to do what she could, it wasn't the same. Trinity will never know the love of her mother. I'd hate for Zoe to grow up the same way."

His words touched her in a way she'd never been touched before, slamming into her heart with a force that made it ache and swell at the same time. No one had ever cared for her the way Chase did. She'd never had anyone take her side this way. Certainly no one, not even her friends, had ever faced up to their own demons to help her out.

"You're one of a kind, Chase Calhoun. I think they broke the mold when they made you. It's incredibly sexy."

His bright blue gaze, so perfectly matched with his polo shirt, captured hers and held. There was no point resisting when the only words she could find would be better off put into action. Charlie raised her arms around his neck, one hand in his hair, leaned into his chest and pressed her lips to his. His mouth opened in surprise and she took advantage of the moment to put her soul into the kiss—every ounce of gratitude, every grain of respect she held for him, and a piece of her heart she'd never given to anyone else.

In that kiss, it didn't matter if he wanted forever or not, or if he was only offering friendship and support. It mattered that, with every action, every gesture, every kiss, she fell a little deeper, grew a little more. Loved him for lighting her path, for helping her make her future and Zoe's achievable without controlling it for her.

His arms tightened around her, holding her closer still, until every surface of their bodies touched, melting into each other as his hands explored her back and hers kept him where she needed him most. Time, surroundings, ghosts, memories, and challenges faded. All she could see and feel, and inhale was Chase. All she knew was that, with him, she was complete. One whole new person. A dangerous, scary thought when everything could still come crashing down and her fairy tale could turn into a nightmare.

"STEADY ON, PYRO. He's not a Lamborghini you can set alight, and the fire extinguisher is on the other side of the room. I'll never get to it in time to put out the flames, for God's sake."

Mason, the voice of reason and his annoying middle brother, had Chase drawing back reluctantly from Charlie's kiss. He wanted to throw her over his shoulder and carry her up those stairs, find the back seat of the Charger and lose himself in her sweet taste. But that would be irresponsible madness. He cast a glance Mason's way. A can of beans in one hand and a spoon in the other, his brother returned his look with one that asked, *"What are you waiting for?"*

"Butt out, Mason."

"Fine. Take it upstairs, kids. There's a box of condoms in row A, on the top shelf next to the bucket of bolts."

Chase sighed. "I don't even want to know why that is, but maybe you should take your own advice sometime."

Mason spooned some of the contents of the can into his mouth and chewed, one eyebrow pitched and a wicked gleam in his eye. If he didn't know better, Chase would think his brother had finally gotten over Paige and moved on. Except he knew that the box of condoms hadn't been touched since Paige left town and no girl other than Charlie had been back here in a long time. Not since the night of Mitch's accident. And the teasing gleam in Mason's eyes was a cover-up for the pain of guilt.

"And give up the freedom to do what I want? Oh, hell no." But he looked into the rapidly emptying can instead of at Chase, which shouted that every word that passed his lips was a lie. He dropped the spoon into the can and raised it in a toast. "You kids go and have fun up there with the dust mites. Watch out for any stray fox squirrels. I hear fall is the perfect time for them to gather nuts."

Charlie reached out and tugged hard at Mason's hair. "Brat."

He rubbed the spot and shot her an injured look. "Ow. What was that for?"

"You need me to make a list? Go help your dad. He's trying to take that tailgate off your pickup by himself. You don't want him getting hurt, do you?"

"No, ma'am." Mason snapped a cheeky salute of compliance in her direction.

Chase shook his head. In a short space of time, Charlie had made a big difference in their lives. His father had a new spring in his step despite the disease beginning to restrict his movements. Mason had made progress Chase had never thought possible, and Molly—sweet some days, gruff the next—had been reduced to a cooing puddle of grandmother-ly softness over the soft bundle of blankets that was Zoe. He didn't want to think about the change she'd brought to him or how good she felt in his arms.

"Great," Mason mumbled good-naturedly as he walked away. "Now I have two mothers telling me what to do."

But the quirk of his smile took the heat out of Mason's words. She'd changed all of them. In that moment, the memories in the attic no longer hurt, the guilt and blame of the accident Mason carried with him daily, dissipated. And the pain of eventually losing their father too seemed almost bearable. Brought about by a girl who'd thumbed her nose at the world. He couldn't imagine Charlotte the rebel, when all he saw was Charlie, his green-eyed girl who'd crept into their lives and done more in a week for them than the whole town had tried to do for years. Mason turned and walked away. Charlie tugged on Chase's shirt for attention and he gave it to her with a smile and touch to her cheek.

"Are you sure you're not a witch?"

She laughed. "It is on the list of things I've been called." Then she tugged on his hand. "Come on, let's go upstairs."

This time there was no hesitation in his step, no memories swirling in his head making his feet heavy and his heart ache. Only Charlie, ahead of him, all curves, tight denim, and perfumed goodness, messing with his concentration and raising a different ache entirely.

At the top of the stairs, she turned to him. "Which way and what am I looking for?"

His gaze went to the top shelf of row A and the box next to the bucket of bolts. He looked back at her with a goofy grin that earned him a slap on the arm before he answered, "Two rows down, middle shelf, the box marked 'legal bullshit'." He held up his hands in defense. "Dad's labeling skills, not mine. I guess that's what he thought of the whole case."

"What was she like, Chase? Your mom."

He closed his eyes to picture her. "Sweet. Funny. Strict. She had to be with four boys and a girl so close together in age—me, Mason, then the twins, Grace and Carter, then Mitch. Only a few months after Mitch was born, she got pregnant again. Too soon, but she was so happy when she found out, it didn't matter."

"How come you lived here above the garage and not at the ranch like you all do now?"

"Dad was away a lot while he was still racing. This was all still a dream he was building. He figured it was easier for her to be closer to town with small children and a baby on the way. It was also more convenient when he came home so that he could spend time with the family while he worked on his custom builds without driving to and from the ranch."

"Makes perfect sense, doesn't it?"

"Does it though?" He ran his hand along the rim of the cardboard box. "If we'd stayed at the ranch, she wouldn't have fallen down the stairs, she wouldn't have had the injuries she did, and we'd still have a mother."

Charlie placed her hand over his to still the movement. "You don't know that for sure, Chase. Accidents happen anywhere."

He refused to look at her. "It was my fault she fell."

"What do you mean?"

He leaned his forehead against the cool steel of the racks, his arm above his head. "She'd nagged us to tidy up that day.

149

She wasn't feeling well. The pregnancy made her tired, more so as she got near the end of it. She'd suffered morning sickness from start to finish. Her blood iron levels were too low, she was on vitamins and medication, lacked energy. When she went to lie down, I got distracted by the television and forgot all about cleaning up like she asked me to." He raised his head. "She got up to go to the bathroom downstairs. She tripped over the toys at the top of the landing and fell. I heard her scream, found her at the bottom of the staircase, curled up in pain, battered by the metal steps, a gash in her head and blood and fluid pooling around her." The memory of finding her that way flickered in his head, a horror movie frozen in that scene.

Charlie's arms came around him, her body warming his back, her face pressed between his shoulder blades. "Oh, Chase!"

"I did what I could, but it was too late." He turned and let her hug him closer, feeling the comfort of her warmth against him as ice chilled his blood. "The doctor said she was already in labor when she fell, not that it changed anything. She'd hit her head hard going down and fractured her skull. Epidural hematoma. Even if she'd lived, she'd have had no quality of life hooked up to life support. It was a miracle that Trinity survived."

"That's so sad. But just like what happened with Mitch, it was an accident. And I know hearing that won't make you feel better, but, God, I hope that one day you'll believe it and forgive yourself. How old were you?"

"I'd just turned ten."

She hugged him harder, her cheek to his chest. "If only we could go back in time and change things. I don't know how to fix you, Chase."

He held her tight, her hair smelling like fresh apples as he pressed his lips to it and felt the goodness of Charlie steer the sad memories away. He had an uncanny feeling his mother was smiling. "I think you may already have."

Chapter Twelve

CHARLIE EASED OUT of Chase's arms. She couldn't stay there, no matter how much she wanted to. There was too much at stake to let herself get lost in him. At least she'd given him some small comfort. It had to be enough. She turned and made her way through the rows until she found the box they were looking for. She traced Marty's strong writing with her finger.

"You'd raise old memories to help me? This wouldn't have been a happy time for your family."

"Even though I was too young to understand most of it, I knew we couldn't let the authorities separate us. That would have finished Dad off for sure. Lucky we had Molly to help." He smiled as he reached for the box. "Molly was a spirited being back then. She still is. And very protective of us. She's fielded some nasty gossip from the locals over the years on our behalf."

"She's sweet. Zoe seems to like her."

Chase lifted the box down. "Yeah, she's a treasure. Come on, let's see if there's anything in here to help us." He nodded toward the stairs. "Be careful going down, okay."

Charlie smiled. "How about you go first? That way if I

fall, I have something to land on."

Chase laughed, the sound coming from deep in his chest as it wiped the sadness from his eyes. "Deal."

She followed him into the office and watched as he lifted the lid on the past. She couldn't begin to imagine the pain the memories would raise for Marty, and for Chase.

"Are you sure your dad is okay with this?" Charlie shifted on her feet.

"It was his idea."

"Thank you. You have a unique family. Not many people would be prepared to help me out."

"This is a different world, honey." He pulled out a bundle of papers, yellowed around the edges. "You're different too."

Charlie smiled, her heart lifting a little. "I guess I have changed."

"You only need to look around you to see the difference you've made here." He pointed out the window into the garage. "There's a sight I'd never thought I'd see again. That's proof right there of how much you've changed."

She looked up from the box to see Mason helping his father take the lining out of the back of the pickup. "He's working on it."

"Yeah. Before you showed him that sketch, Mason wouldn't even look at the pickup unless it was to take the annual hammer to it. That night we went up the hill, something shifted for all of us. We all kinda took a step forward."

"You can't think a simple sketch could have changed anything for you?"

"You have a talent, Charlie. You capture more than you realize in your art. You interpret things through it that no one has ever achieved before. Mason recognized something in that design that resonated with him, that flicked a switch we haven't been able to activate. You did that. The design you did for Carter? We'd tried a few artists and not one of them was able to capture the essence and spirit in the purpose of the ranch. Yet you took one look and created the perfect design. That's a gift."

"Thank you." She reached up to kiss his cheek. "I wish my father could see it that way."

"He will. Once word gets around you're designing for us, we'll have to fight to keep you. Everyone will want a Charlotte Jackson design." He slipped his arm around her for a quick hug just as the laptop on the desk alerted him to a call coming in. "That's Trinity. I bet she'll want one too."

Charlie shifted to move away as he clicked on the answer icon, but his hold on her tightened gently as if he wasn't quite ready to let her go. Uncertainty snaked through her. If Chase's sister recognized her and talked about it in track circles, her father would know exactly where she was rather than a location near the closest satellite tower. But the chances of recognition were slim when she looked a lot different now. She couldn't hide forever. And if Trinity was coming home any time soon, her cover would be blown anyway.

"Hello, Mother." Trinity's grin filled the screen before she backed up, so they could see her face in full. "Oh, and hello pretty blonde girl. Chase Calhoun, have you been holding out on me? When did you find yourself a girlfriend?"

"Oh ... we're not ... I'm not ..." What was she to him exactly? A friend? An employee?

"Hey, brat. A bit more respect for my very talented design artist, thanks."

Trinity snorted and pushed her racing suit down to her waist. "That's why you're hugging her?"

"If you could see her work, you'd hug her too. Trinity, meet Charlie. Charlie, this is my baby sister. She's the one currently terrorizing NASCAR drivers nationwide."

"And beating them too." Trinity peered into the screen. "Wait a minute. You look familiar. Have we met before?"

"No." *Not exactly the truth, Charlotte.* There had been that one time. At the same party where she'd set Ronan's car alight. Charlie crossed her fingers and prayed.

"Oh. My. God." Trinity's eyes widened in recognition, excitement threading through her voice. "I almost didn't recognize you without the purple hair, piercings, and black leather. Charlotte Jackson, do you know your father is looking everywhere for you? He has every police precinct on high alert, there's a private detective out there somewhere trying to track you down, and a psychiatrist on standby to have you committed. Your father's claiming you've had a complete mental breakdown and that you're dangerous. The gossip's all over the team refreshment tent."

"Trinity, please tell me you're calling from somewhere private." Chase's hold on Charlie loosened, his forehead drawing down into a frown.

She held her breath, anger clutching at her chest, her mind unwilling to believe her father would go to such lengths to discredit her.

"My trailer. Paige is here though." She peered into the screen again. "Wow, you don't look crazy, Charlotte."

"Trinity, I'm swearing you and Paige to secrecy. You can't tell anyone where Charlie is, okay?"

"No way. Her brother is a sanctimonious asshole and her father is a rude, obnoxious pig."

Charlie winced.

"Still, show a little respect, brat," Chase scolded his sister. "We might not like what he's doing, but he is still Charlie's father."

"You're right. Sorry, Charlotte. It just irks me that he can say the things he's saying, and people will believe it because it comes from the mouth of the great Tony Jackson. I've been issued a penalty in this heat because Ronan and Tony are claiming I made a false start. He says I was already rolling when the flag went up. They're reviewing it now."

"That doesn't sound good." Chase leaned forward, his hands on either side of the laptop, his hip brushing Charlie's leg.

She should move away, but his warmth gave her comfort. Ronan wouldn't hold back. He was a sore loser. "I'm sorry,

Trinity."

"Not your fault, honey. I'll deal with him. Not quite in the same way you dealt with his Lamborghini, but, hey, I've got a few tricks up my sleeve to show him who is the better driver." She laughed. "I'm really curious to know how you came to be hiding in my father's garage, though."

Charlie smiled at Chase. "Long story."

Chase smiled back, his gaze holding hers, his hand at her back before he turned his face to the screen again. "One we're not going to go into with you right now, brat."

"Oh!" Trinity drew the word out. "It's like that, is it? Ha."

"Mind your own business. What did you call for anyway?"

"To talk to my brother-mother. I miss you guys."

"So, come home then. You know that's what Dad would like."

"I've promised Paige we'll see out this season. This business with Ronan Jackson is getting ugly, Chase." The smile slipped from Trinity's face. "He's doing some pretty nasty stuff out there on the track."

A cold shiver stole down Charlie's spine. Her brother had done some rotten things off the track in the past, but he'd never let that flow on over into his driving before. "What do you mean by nasty?"

"Nudging, sideswiping, pushing other drivers off the track. The problem is he's good at hiding the moves, especially when he's in the pack. I'm sorry, Charlotte, I know he's family."

Charlie shook her head. "Don't apologize. But be careful, please. My brother doesn't know where to draw the line. Have you reported it to the officials?"

"We've tried, but the claims have been dismissed. He's an overconfident ass now that he knows he can get away with it. I think his false start allegations are payback."

Charlie chewed on her bottom lip, far too familiar with Ronan's brand of payback. It would be cruel, nasty, and even dangerous. Not a good thing when a driver would be doing more than two hundred miles per hour on a track where the smallest mistake could cause a spectacular crash. Not when that crash could cause injury or death. Not something she'd wish on her worst enemy, let alone someone as sweet as Trinity. And hadn't the Calhouns suffered enough?

The poisonous tentacles of Jackson vendettas could reach far and the harm it could do would be life-altering. Anger fused with concern. She couldn't let this escalate to a point where there'd be loss or harm to the family she'd come to love. Damage done by a family who cared for nothing other than victory. Whichever way they took it.

CHASE WATCHED CHARLIE work in silence. Ever since ending the call with Trinity, she'd been quiet and withdrawn. He didn't mind admitting to being a little edgy himself. Knowing Ronan Jackson was a bit of a loose cannon on the track hadn't set his mind at ease at all. Nor Charlie's, it seemed.

"What's eating Pyro?" Mason nudged his shoulder, a peanut butter and jelly sandwich between his paws. "She's been pretty quiet this afternoon."

"You mean besides you trying to scare her shitless with a sledgehammer?"

Mason had the good sense to look sheepish. "Yeah, sorry about that. It won't happen again."

Chase raised an eyebrow. "Is that a promise?"

"Something clicked back into place today." Mason shrugged. "Not quite sure what it means yet, but I'm working on it. What's going on in Charlotte's world?"

"There's some serious family trouble happening. Trinity says track gossip is that her father is trying to have her diagnosed as mentally unfit."

"You're not serious?" He whistled. "Pleasant family. Can't say I've seen anything that makes me think she's unstable."

"You mean other than having the nuts to approach you in a rage when you have a weapon in your hands?" Chase pinched the bridge of his nose to stay the pain where a headache bloomed behind his eyes.

"You know the only thing I ever wanted to smash was that damn pickup truck." He shifted his feet. "And I don't want to do that anymore, so she's safe."

"I'm not so sure about that. I'm a little worried about her brother." He filled Mason in on what Trinity had told him about Ronan Jackson's threats. "It concerns me that the track officials appear to be ignoring his dangerous behavior in a race. That's playing with lives."

"Do you think Dad should call someone higher up and talk to them about it? Maybe I shouldn't put that sledge-hammer away just yet. If he so much as looks at Trinity the wrong way, he's gonna feel the full force of the Calhoun wrath."

"I'll talk to Dad and see what he can do."

Mason slapped a hand on Chase's shoulder. "Go get 'em, Mother. By the way, Molly called. She says there's a dodgy-looking rental car parked outside her shop. She spotted it on her way back over."

Chase shoved his hands into his pockets and made sure Zoe was safe and snug in her porta-crib in the corner of the office. "Could be the private detective Trinity mentioned. Charlie's father hired one to find her."

Mason chewed on his sandwich as he processed Chase's words. "I don't get it. Why do that to your own child? Unless Charlotte is a damn good actress and has us all fooled?"

"You don't believe that and neither do I. And if anyone can pick a liar, it's Dad. He would have said something if he thought she was lying to us."

"You really like this girl, don't you?"

His father said something to Charlie to that made her smile, a sweet, gentle tip of her lips full of affection. Not the same smile that lit up the room and made his heart pound, his mind blur, and his lips want to steal it from her mouth. He wanted to believe she saved *that* smile for him alone. "I don't like to see people treated unfairly."

Mason laughed. "Sure, that's all it is. You keep telling yourself that. So, all those little touches, secret smiles…" He leaned closer. "All those *un-motherly*-like reactions—they're all just for show?"

Irritation skittered along his nerve ends. Sometimes Chase wanted to swat his brother like an annoying fly. "Shut up, Mason. Eat your sandwich."

His brother's annoyingly knowing grin only grew wider. "I think I might go across the road and play with our mystery visitor outside Molly's."

Anger rose and flashed in Chase's eyes. "Don't you dare do anything stupid that will get Charlie into any more trouble than she's already in. Stay out of it, Mason."

"And you say you don't care. While you think about that, I'm going to check out the ratbag in the car and make sure he's just a tourist. Give him a nice warm, Bigfork welcome. In the meanwhile, you might want to start digging through that box and see what you can come up with to protect your girlfriend and her kid."

"She's not my girlfriend. And I'm coming with you to check out the tourist."

"If he is a private eye, he's pretty dumb to get himself spotted." Mason finished his sandwich and dusted imaginary crumbs from his hands. "Or maybe he wants Charlie to know he's there."

Irritation with his brother morphed into wariness. "Like a threat."

"Or intimidation." Mason shrugged.

"Having heard what Trinity said about the family, that sounds exactly like something they'd stoop to." Chase frowned as Charlie took a call on her phone, the scowl that drew her brows down quickly followed by her hanging up on the caller. She wiped her hands on her coveralls and headed toward the door into the showroom. "What is she doing?"

"Looks like she has the same thing in mind as we have. To make our mystery visitor welcome."

"Damn it. Let's go." Chase crossed the floor with urgent strides.

"Right behind you."

"Dad, could you stay here and keep an eye on Zoe?" He acknowledged his father's nod before calling out, "Charlie, wait up."

Chase's stomach clenched as she ignored him. He followed her onto the street where Charlie wrenched open the door on the rental sedan.

"You can turn this car around and go right back the way you came, Ed. And when you get there, you can tell my father to go to hell."

"Did you seriously think you could give me the slip?" He pointed to his cell phone in the cradle on the dashboard. "Tracking apps are amazing things. Should never have turned your phone on. Get your things and get in the car. I don't want to have to make you."

"The only thing you can *make*, Ed, is the drive-through lane at the burger joint. I'm not going anywhere with you and I'm not going home."

"Still haven't learned not to sass, Charlotte. Your father's got me on the clock and he's docking my pay for every minute of that time you waste. I don't like losing that kind of money over a snot-nosed brat like you."

"Then tell him to man up and do his own dirty work."

"Pretty brave outside of your daddy's jurisdiction, aren't you?" He made a grab for her wrist as she stepped back out of reach.

Chase stepped in next to her, placed his hands on his hips, feet apart, braced for anything. "Do we have a problem here, Charlie?"

"Because we don't mind taking care of trouble." Mason leaned against the rear door, arms folded, feet crossed at the ankles, deceptively casual, but inside, his brother would be a tightly coiled clock spring, waiting to act if the guy in the car so much as sneezed in the wrong direction.

"Nothing I can't handle. Ed here was about to head out of town and I wanted to give him a message to take away with him."

Chase studied the man in the driver's seat, his hands white-knuckled on the steering wheel, eyes hidden behind reflective lenses under the brim of a baseball cap as he stared ahead and refused to look at them. "This is your father's PI? Not very imaginative in his disguise, is he? Didn't even try to blend in."

"Lazy," Mason agreed.

"I think you picked the wrong tourist season, Ed." Chase folded his arms. "You should come back in the summer. The fishing is much better then."

"I'm only doing my job," Sullivan snarled.

"Then maybe it's time you considered a career change." Chase leaned down and stared at the man's profile. "If you're not out of town within the next ten minutes, Sheriff Hutchins will be asked to escort you to the outer limits."

"Based on what? I've done nothing wrong. I'm outside a grocery store. I could be picking up supplies."

Chase peered into the confines of the sedan. "With a laptop running spyware, a set of binoculars on the seat and wearing…" He sniffed the air. "The smell of someone who hasn't had a shower in a few days? I hope antiperspirant is on your list. Get out of town, Sullivan. And don't come back." He straightened and stepped away from the car.

"See you, Ed. Tell my father if he wants to see me, it will be on my terms not his." Charlie slammed the door shut.

They stood back as Sullivan pulled away from the curb, made a U-turn, and then watched the tail end of the car disappear down the street.

"Well, that went well." Mason sounded almost disappointed.

"We can't be sure he's gone." Chase shook his head.

Unease trickled down his spine. People like Ed Sullivan and Tony Jackson wouldn't give up that easily. If they'd come this far across the country to find her, who knew where they'd set the boundaries.

He turned to Charlie. "Are you okay?"

"I'm fine." She looked at him. "Thank you for the back-up. Ed can be pretty nasty."

He drew her closer with an arm around her waist. "You scared me going in alone like that." She turned into him, so he gave in to temptation and wrapped her in his hold, securing her tightly against him.

"I wouldn't have taken the risk if I thought Ed was a physical threat. He's sneaky, underhanded, and nasty, which makes him dangerous at confrontation level. I need to be smarter than him. Get to my father before he does." She shivered. "And that means I have to make a phone call. The one I've been avoiding because it's too soon."

"So, it wasn't your father who called you a few minutes ago?"

Charlie's hands tightened on his hips. "No, that was Ed letting me know he was parked across the road, waiting for me."

"Too lazy to even get out of the car."

She laid her cheek against his chest. "I'm glad I had the advantage of that. He freaks me out. He's a slippery toad, that guy. Which is exactly why my father keeps him on staff."

The wind cut a chill down the street. People moved in and out of Molly's place, bags in hand, cutting them a passing glance. The gossip mill would be running hot at the checkout with everyone wondering what was going down.

Mason walked back across the street to the garage, leaving them standing alone in the space left by Ed's rental car.

"So what now, Charlie? You can't hide anymore if they know where you are." Would she run again? Find another town, another state to hide in?

She turned her face up to his, determination in her eyes. "I'm going to call my father and settle this right now."

And because the determination and fire inside her was so damn sexy, he tipped up her chin, and kissed her in the middle of the main street, which would no doubt have the gossip mill turning for days. He only cared that Charlie kissed him back.

Chapter Thirteen

E D SULLIVAN. HER father would only send that filthy, slimy scumbag. A man not afraid to lie, to manufacture rumors to achieve his goal. In the privacy of Chase's office with Zoe safely in her arms, Charlie pulled her phone out of her pocket and dialed, her spine stiff as she waited for her father to answer.

"Charlotte. I hope you're cooperating with Ed."

"How dare you?" Anger, hot and sharp, made every muscle in her body tense at the bored tone in his voice.

"I don't know what you mean, Charlotte. If you weren't so damn stubborn and rebellious, I wouldn't have to hire someone to bring you home."

"It didn't occur to you to come and find me yourself?"

"I don't play your little games of hide and seek, Charlotte. I have a job to do. I don't have the time or patience for your attention seeking."

"You think that's what this is about? Attention seeking?" Hadn't she expected it? All her life she'd fought to earn their love and affection, their praise and pride, but they'd never been able to see past Ronan and never would. The time had come to stop fighting for it, to fight for something far more precious. To follow her own path in life, ready or not. "Call your dog off. I'm not coming back. I'm an adult and I make my own choices."

"You're a disturbed adult who is no more than a child in her head. Your record is more than proof of that. Get in that car with Ed."

"I'm not going anywhere alone with that disgusting man."

"Are we really going to go down the track of that lie again?"

Pain, sharp as a knife, speared her chest. "A lie? He propositioned me, *Dad*. If I performed sexual favors for him, he wouldn't slander my name all over social media. Do you remember that? I told him where to go and the next day, there were pictures of me all over the Internet."

"Pictures taken when you were passed out drunk on the streets."

"Pictures photoshopped to make it look like I was drunk, passed out on the street. Pictures taken without my knowledge or permission. And did you try to stop it? No!" All the old hurt of being called a liar resurfaced. That her parents had believed Ed's story over hers. That her father had kept him on his payroll even though she had recorded proof of Ed's propositions to her. He'd refused to listen to them, putting it down to more of her attention-seeking behavior.

"Enough! You will come home, Charlotte. You will hand over that baby for adoption to the couple I've chosen, and you will resume your position on the marketing team as if none of this ever happened."

"I'm Zoe's mother. I'm not giving her away."

"You have no choice in the matter, Charlotte. You hand that baby over or I'll have you declared mentally incompetent and unfit to take care of a child."

"Why is this so important to you? I've always been invisible to you until now. Why the sudden focus?"

"You always have to make it about you, don't you?" His anger vibrated through the phone.

"This isn't about me." Her anger surged to match his. "It's about my child. A living, breathing human being you want to give away like some discarded memento that's causing you embarrassment with its memory."

"I have a family lined up, ready to hand over five million dollars for that baby. Do you have any idea how much that money will mean to your brother's career?"

Shock, colder than the wind that sliced down the street outside, froze the blood in her veins and robbed her lungs of air. "You *sold* my baby?" The sharp edge of the desk dug into her thighs as the impact of his words hit. "You *bastard*."

"I want that money, Charlotte. Ronan needs a new car next season, and Leroy Diego has the funds to sponsor it in return for the baby his wife so desperately wants."

"Then maybe Ronan needs to work harder at developing his skills and winning some races." A flood of emotions rushed through her.

Disbelief warred with anger, disappointment fought with regret. Regret that her father would never be the perfect grandfather. That he'd never care for Zoe the way she did. That all hope he might change his mind once he got to know her had been squashed by his actions.

"My baby is not for sale."

"You might want to think a little harder on that, Charlotte. I don't know what crazy scheme you had in mind that made you choose to run to Montana. But choosing the Calhouns for cover was a big mistake."

"The Calhouns have nothing to do with it. I didn't choose to run to them. I hadn't planned to come to Bigfork. Leave them out of it. This is between you and me. No one else."

"Not anymore, Charlotte. You've given me the perfect leverage. I give you two days to find your way home."

"And if I don't?" She recognized the tone coated with the underlying threat of consequences. She wanted to ignore it, to think he couldn't touch her anymore, but that would be foolish when her father was the master of manipulation.

"Trinity Calhoun will have a very hard time staying on the track in the next race and Ed will go live with the story that Chase Calhoun pushed his mother down the stairs and killed her."

Silence screamed from the phone in her hand as her father hung up, his betrayal a hot blade that ripped at her heart. She eased down to the carpet and sat with her back against the desk, holding Zoe tight against her heart.

She could hand Zoe over to Ed and keep moving. Turn her back on the Jacksons forever. Leave Bigfork and the chance at making her dream come true, move away from the Calhouns and a future that might even promise happiness someday. Away from Chase. She couldn't reconcile her thoughts to a life without Zoe. The notion cracked her heart wide open. Her father would have what he wanted, Ronan would win again, Zoe would have strangers for parents, and the Calhouns would remain untouched. There'd only be one loser in the game.

A loser was something she never wanted to be again, but could she find the courage to expose her father's actions, start an all-out, highly-publicized war with the potential to touch the Calhouns and put another family member's life at risk? Because her father wouldn't hesitate to use the media to his advantage or carry out his threat and all she had was hearsay. No proof other than the threat that rang in her mind, nothing concrete she could take to the authorities.

Zoe waved a fist in the air and Charlie captured it, pressing her lips to the baby soft skin. She'd come this far, fought hard for her freedom. She wouldn't give up the fight now, not when she had so much more to lose and the Calhouns didn't deserve the damage Ed Sullivan could do inventing lies.

CHASE STOOD IN the doorway, watching Charlie as she cuddled Zoe close. Pushing away from the frame, he moved to kneel in front of her, noted her frown and slipped a finger under her chin to lift it. "Hey."

She raised her eyes to his. "Hey."

"What's going on?"

"My father threatened you and your family."

"I'd like to hear how so I can nail his ass to the wall. Tell me what he said." He sat beside her against the desk and placed his arm around her, pulling her close.

"He's given me an ultimatum. If I don't return home in two days, he'll leak a story to the press that you were responsible for your mom's fall. I can't let him do that to you, Chase. Dig up dirt that isn't true to sling it at you when you don't deserve it. Your family has suffered enough. I'm his target."

Tension seized his shoulders. The same old rip of pain tore at his heart at the mention of his mother. His mom's life had been cut short too early, yes, but he wouldn't let the likes of Tony Jackson and Ed Sullivan taint her memory. "Your father won't be saying anything that hasn't already been a fleeting thought in people's minds. Our proof that my mom's fall was an accident is the coroner's report. The police ruled out any foul play. A woman alone with five small children, living in an attic. No sign of forced entry. Nothing to indicate a struggle. The only perpetrator a toy train she asked me to put away and I didn't. No one's going to believe your father's lies. Not anymore. But I wish so hard some days that I could change things. Bring her back somehow."

Charlie leaned her head on his shoulder. "She is here every day." She tapped his chest above his heart. "It was an accident. You need to forgive yourself, and if I let my father do what he's threatening to do, you'll never be able to let go." She turned her face up to his. "I did this. I need to fix it. Zoe's welfare is at stake. So many people could get hurt when my father starts slinging mud. I won't let him sully your mom's memory by trying to make it something it wasn't. Nor will I let him hurt Mason, not when he's on the path to recovery. And your dad ... he doesn't deserve to be the loser in this."

He hated the crack in her words that forced him to look at her, the hurt that made a frown form on her brow and the inner turmoil that made her lips tighten. He gave her leg an encouraging rub and let his hand rest on her thigh. He didn't want this trouble on his doorstep when his father's health and the business should be his priority.

He hadn't needed the complication that was Charlotte Jackson or the trouble she'd brought with her. Yet she'd found him. In a place where he'd suffered his own losses and pain. She'd brought light and change and happiness with her. She'd made the dark, sad memories of the attic bright again. Made him realize that from bad came good sometimes.

"Chase?" His name whispered between them.

"No point wasting more time, Charlie." Foreboding snaked its way through him to stiffen the muscles in his neck and between his shoulder blades. "You'll have our support. A Calhoun never goes back on his word. We'll work something out."

"I can't let them take her. I understand they can afford to take good care of her if they've got that kind of money, but they're still strangers. This won't be straightforward. If I don't give Zoe up, my father stands to lose five million dollars."

Disbelief made Chase's fingers tighten on her thigh. "Wait a minute. Are you saying that in return for Zoe, the adoptive parents will pay your father five million dollars?"

Charlie nodded, tears spilling over onto her cheeks.

"He'd sell your baby." It wasn't a question. It was a statement that ripped out his heart as he looked at the baby now cuddled tightly to her chest.

Her voice was barely a whisper in the office. "He's also threatened to have Trinity forced off the track in the next race. That's bordering on insanity. My father's always been a hard man, but this … it's unforgiveable."

Anger seared his thoughts. Who the hell did Tony Jackson think he was, threatening his family? Threatening anyone? "That's one thing that won't happen. I'll get onto Trinity's team manager and warn him since she's already mentioned your brother's erratic behavior on the track. We'll pull her out of the race if we need to. She's not going to like it, but she'll deal with it." He reached up to the desktop behind him and pulled down a box of tissues, pulled one out and handed it to Charlie. "We've got this, honey."

"I'm not sure we have. If we expose him for his threats and this deal, the fallout will be huge. I have nothing except a verbal threat. Ed will rake up everything he can to throw back at us and he has plenty of documented evidence to feed the media with. Including Mitch's accident and Mason's role in it. We need to stop them."

Scenarios unfolded in his mind of how things would play out when the story hit the gossip rags and filtered onto social media. People, hungry for drama, desperate to immerse themselves in the tragic lives of others, would drive that story into the spotlight and rip the Band-Aids off wounds that had only now begun to heal.

The impact it would have on Mason, who'd only just started to forgive himself, to emerge from the darkness of depression and guilt that had held him captive for too long. The pain it would resurrect for everyone, including Paige who, like Mason, still believed the accident was as much her fault as anyone's.

Carter, Grace, and his father—how much faster would his dad's health deteriorate if his life's work was ripped away by the lies that might be told? Because people believed everything they read or were told. Guilty until proven innocent. And just like that, everything they'd worked for would come crashing down with the same force as the sledgehammer Mason used on the pickup every year.

Chase wiped a hand over his face and sighed. "I have to do everything I can to protect my family and keep them safe. I'll call our lawyer, Frank Mahoney, and get him to work on the legalities of placing an embargo on all press releases pertaining to Calhoun family private business, but we need to make sure Trinity has protection first."

"I have no proof of his threats or the offer of money for the adoption."

"So, we catch him red-handed." All he could see was the devastation and hurt in Charlie's eyes. Chase pressed his lips to her hair. "I'm pretty sure selling a baby is illegal in all states. I can't believe he'd do that to you."

"I haven't exactly given him reason to believe I would be a good mother to Zoe. Maybe he's right."

"He's wrong. Dead wrong. Anyone can see how much you love that baby."

"Sometimes love just isn't enough." Charlie curled her fingers into his shirt. "This is my mess. I must fix it. I just have to find a way to do that without hurting you and your family any more than I may have already."

"You can't give her up, Charlie." He'd adopt Zoe himself before he'd let Tony Jackson sell her like some unwanted commodity that wasn't even his to sell.

"Giving her up is one thing. Selling her is whole other ball game." She shivered against him. "I can't believe he'd sink that low."

"My offer still stands."

"To marry you? That would only make my father even more determined to destroy you. He wants that money. He's hungry for a win that will take TRJ Racing to the top of the scoreboard. It's all he's ever cared about."

Chase hugged her tightly. "I wish things could have been different for you."

"All I wanted was for him to see me. For the first few months alone in the Hamptons, I seriously considered adoption, to do what he wanted me to. But once Zoe started to move, she became real to me. Then, when she was born, I knew I couldn't give her away. I had to change, take a stand against him." Releasing her grip on his shirt, her fingers traced a pattern on his chest. "I'm done trying to make him love me."

Chase cupped her chin in his hand and lifted her face, so she could meet his gaze. "More fool him. There's a lot to love about you, Charlotte Jackson, and I'd like you and Zoe to stick around. We're in this together now." Then his mouth descended on hers and he lost himself in the taste of her lips.

Chapter Fourteen

DARKNESS SETTLED OUTSIDE the cabin window, the rain tapping out a beat on the roof. Charlie stretched the kinks out of her spine as Chase tossed another log on the fire. Light flickered off the walls in the great room. She loved this room with its marshmallow sofas and wool rugs, the flames leaping up the chimney of the stone fireplace, and the peaceful surroundings.

Here there was peace, a sense of belonging, and a man she was fast falling head over heels for. He'd worked for hours, going over old adoption court cases, checking legalities, confirming rights, looking for loopholes they could close if her father decided to use them. Scattered memories of his own father's battle to keep his children lay on the floor in front of them.

"So..." He sat down next to her again and stretched out his legs, his hip touching hers. "In Dad's case, my paternal grandparents tried to claim adoption rights based on that my grandmother had taken care of us for six weeks while Dad sorted out Mom's funeral and estate. The law states that they could claim adoption if they'd taken care of us in a guardianship role."

"Why would they want to do that?"

Chase's shoulder rubbed against hers as he shrugged. "I guess they figured Dad couldn't raise six kids alone. Trinity and Grace were their biggest concern, especially with Trinity being a newborn and all."

Charlie curled her fingers around his where his hand rested on his thigh. "They cared."

"They thought they were doing the right thing. Dad didn't quite see it that way at the time. It caused a rift in the family, but when it went to court, he won the case for custody. My grandparents retired to Sarasota and Dad stayed out of contact for a while. Then Grandad had a heart attack and Dad took us all to see him."

"They settled their differences?" She wished her story would have the same happy outcome. That she'd read her father wrong, that her mother wasn't cold and distant, and that her brother wasn't a puppet of terror tied to the end of her father's strings.

"It took a while, but they got there in the end. After that, they spent some time up here in the summer with us and they could see Dad had it under control." He smiled, his dimple creasing his cheek. "He worked extra hard to prove it too. Nan didn't find a single speck of dust or a can out of order in the pantry."

Charlie squeezed his fingers. "I'm glad they made their peace."

He turned his head to hers, his mouth a whisper away from her lips. "I hope you find peace too."

"I think I have. All I need to do is jump one last hurdle, but it's one I wish I didn't have to. This time he's gone too far." Any hope she'd had of him changing had evaporated into the stony silence that had followed her father's call.

"Together we'll stop this, Charlie."

She reached up to cup his face between her hands and kissed him lightly. "Thank you." And because he tasted like promise and hope, she kissed him some more.

He turned to her, his lips under hers soft and pliant. Coaxing, inviting, gentle, and unhurried. As if they had all the time in the world to learn each other's flavor. As if no threat waited on the threshold, ready to tear them apart if they failed. As if the baby who lay sleeping in the room next door would always be theirs and they were playing for keeps.

They'd been brought together by a twist of fate, but anything they felt for each other had to be more than just another fling that might dwindle to nothing when the heat subsided. She had Zoe to consider now and if the fight to keep her dragged on for months, maybe years, would Chase have the patience and staying power to see it through? Did he love them enough? Did he love them at all or was this simply attraction that would burn out like the fire in the grate?

Charlie drew away from his kiss, still holding his face. "Where are we going? Us?"

Chase covered her hand with his. "We're taking one step at a time. You've grown on me, you and Zoe. Each day with you, I fall in love a little more. I'd like you beside me in the future, as my wife, my business partner, the mother of our children. And I'll stand beside you in this fight for Zoe every step of the way."

"What if I lose?" She didn't want to think about losing, but money and power often trumped truth and fairness. Judges could be bought, blackmailed, swayed by lies, and misinterpretation of the law.

"You won't lose if we fight this the right way." He drew her hands down and held them, his thumbs stroking across her knuckles. "You know we need to lodge a report with the sheriff about the money your father has been offered for Zoe, right?"

An ache squeezed her heart. Family was family, and, even though her father was on the verge of committing a crime, it still felt like betrayal. No matter how badly he'd treated her, or how much distance and bad blood had come between them, all she'd craved was his acceptance and love. An empty wish fading as fast as the shimmer of heat on the track's surface as it cooled.

"I know. I feel sorry for the Diegos. This will impact them too."

"Honey, the Diegos are accomplices in this. They're prepared to buy a baby under the banner of adoption. They know what they're doing is wrong. Frank will deal with them, find out who instigated the deal. If they approached your father or if he approached them."

"We won't be able to do this without it getting media coverage. It's too big for the gossip rags to ignore and put their own spin on. Big name in NASCAR sells his rebel daughter's baby… they'll dig up my past, rake around in our lives, stir up everything I've tried so hard to leave behind and let settle."

The domino effect it would have until the last tile toppled and ended her brother's career in racing. The damage Ronan could do with his acid tongue when TRJ Racing would be made to roll down the shutters on their pit garage because it wouldn't survive another scandal.

"Then we need to make sure the press gets your side of the story first. We can't stop this from going public, but we can manage how it does. After we've been to see Sheriff Hutchins in the morning to lodge your case, we'll write up a press release. Frank will look it over and ensure that an embargo is placed on anything that doesn't come from sworn statements, tie them up in knots so that the only story that goes live is one that has been thoroughly checked for factual reporting. Make it too hard for them to give too much airtime to the story."

"I wish there was another way." No matter how awful and criminal her father's actions were, she hadn't wanted it to come to this.

Chase ran a hand over her hair, tucking the weight of it behind her ear. "If we can find another way, we will. But I don't think your father will make it any easier for you. The difference is, you don't have to do this alone anymore. Come here, Charlie."

He tugged her onto his lap and wrapped her in his arms.

She settled on his thighs, her head on his shoulder, her body pressed to his chest. His warmth seeped through her, the rub of his thumbs against the wool of her sweater creating a fiery friction of awareness.

She lifted her face to his, caught his gaze as hot as the fire that threw flickering light into the room, watched his lips descend, and closed her eyes to the sensation of them on hers. A light rub of request before she granted him permission and opened her mouth to the unhurried, gentle seduction of his tongue.

With a sigh, she kissed him back, falling into the taste of Chase, a flavor far more addictive than the herbal teas he brewed for her, or the wine he'd served with dinner. A taste so unique, she never wanted anything else. Chase—mother, brother, carer, lover—all of him wrapped up and hers to keep if she wanted him. She wanted him. With every breath, every stroke of his tongue, every whisper of his lips. Right here, in front of the fire, on the soft rug under them.

She wanted to fall, with him, into the comfort of love and promise of forever. Into the reality of a future that promised happiness and fulfillment. And, even if only just for tonight, she wanted to forget about the battle ahead, to feel alive under the hands that slipped under the hem of her sweater and the fingers that trailed her skin.

He whispered words against her neck, so quiet she couldn't hear them only feel them. Then his lips trailed to her collarbone and every nerve ending came alive, sensitive to every touch, responding to every stroke, melting any last remaining thread of resistance and doubt.

His hand cupped her breast, his thumb grazing the budded nipple through the cotton of her feeding bra. He smiled against the pulse in her throat. "Sexier than any silk underwear right now."

His fingers unclipped the hook that held the flap in place and then his palm was warm against her skin, curling around the fullness, stroking with unhurried attention that made her want to urge him on. His body hardened under her. Hers tightened in response. She wanted to straddle him, take him, love him, take that next step forward off the cliff into the unknown. Fly with the sensations his lips and hands created and give him back every ounce of pleasure she knew would come.

"Love me, Chase," she whispered as he nibbled her skin, tiny nips that had her shivering deliciously against him.

"I already do." Then with his hands and words and mouth, he showed her how much.

CHASE WATCHED CHARLIE sleep, curled up against him with her hair spread out on a cushion off the sofa. He couldn't lose her. Not after tonight. Not when he loved her with every fiber of his being. No one had ever touched his heart the way Charlie had. He'd been enchanted by her pretty face in Molly's Old Time Five and Dime, impressed by her talent in the garage, intrigued by her fight to keep what she cared about most, and floored by his need for her. Once would never be enough with Charlie. He wanted her by his side, every day, every night, but the reality of the fallout from what faced them could tear them apart. He was confident she wouldn't lose Zoe, not if they could prove Charlie's father planned to accept money in return for the baby's adoption. But if they couldn't prove the transaction, they'd need a backup plan.

With the doctor's report giving Charlie the all-clear, Tony Jackson couldn't follow his threat of having her declared mentally incompetent. Zoe had a clean bill of health. She'd ticked all the milestones on the development charts. They had a home and security, an income. Would proving Charlie was a good mom be enough to come between a man like Tony and the lure of five million dollars? Chase doubted it.

He dragged the box they'd brought down from the attic closer to him. Under the legal files were memories. Photographs, certificates, race reports. A history of his father's time on the track buried under the weight of his loss.

Beside him, Charlie stirred. He dropped a hand to her hair, enjoying the softness of it against his skin. She smiled in her sleep and snuggled closer. He wanted to wake her, kiss her again, but for now, he'd let her rest. He turned his attention back to the box, flicked through the photographs, lingered on the ones of his mom. He'd always miss her, always regret his mistake, but the raw edge of guilt he'd carried with him since had softened.

He picked up a cream manila folder marked with a date

and location. *Daytona International Speedway. Incident Report.* Chase flicked through the pages until a name leaped off the yellowed pages. Tony Jackson.

Easing away from Charlie so he didn't disturb her sleep, he moved to the kitchen and turned on the light above the breakfast bar. The report was comprehensive. Detailing each move, each statement, each piece of conflicting evidence. The more he read, the wider his smile grew, and when Charlie ran her hands up his back, over his shoulders and around his waist, her cheek pressed to his back, he could turn to her and say, "Baby, I think we've got something."

Charlie stepped into the space between his legs and eyed the open folder. "A race report?"

He grinned. Now he understood what it felt like to win a race. "Leverage. All we need to do is get your father to come to Montana to meet us face-to-face."

"Good luck with that. He'll send Ed back to town or his lawyer, but he'd never come himself."

"I think we can change his mind about that, but it would involve setting some bait."

"Bait?" Charlie frowned. "I'm not sure what would be enough of a lure for him."

Zoe's cry reached down the hall. Chase slipped the file closer to Charlie. "I'll go see to Zoe while you have a read of that. Then we'll talk a plan while Zoe is fed and settles again."

He slipped off the bar chair, her warmth leaving him as he moved away. Under the light, her white-blonde hair shone, her shoulders tense as she read. No matter how bad things were between her and her family, this would hurt. Exposing the extent of her father's cheating to the world would take courage, commitment, tenacity. Things she had in spades. Except this time, she'd have the love and support of a real family when she took her father on, and Chase would be there to catch her if she fell.

Chapter Fifteen

THE WAIT HAD been the killer, but her father had taken the bait. Her call to say she wanted to come to an agreement had worked, and her ultimatum that the deal would be off if he didn't come in person had been surprisingly well received. His way of coming to gloat about his success and put his rebel daughter in her place.

Sheriff Hutchins had taken her statement, run his background checks, and unearthed far more than he'd expected. The Diegos weren't the caring, childless, adoptive parents they'd portrayed themselves as. The more he'd investigated, the more he'd uncovered. The life they'd had planned for Zoe was not one that involved raising her in a loving family and growing her into a stable, successful young adult. Their intentions for her were far more sinister. Intentions that made Charlie feel ill knowing her father had been aware of what would happen to her baby.

Three days after she'd called him to say she was ready to negotiate, he'd arrived. Now he stood inside Calhoun Customs Garage as if he owned the place, confident he'd won, with her brother a step behind him. Still taking direction, an angry puppet as much under Tony Jackson's control as she'd been. Still trying to intimidate her with his threatening stance.

Mason had the situation covered, the thump of a monkey wrench cracking through the tension in the room with every slap against his palm as Chase stepped out of his office into the garage.

"There you are, Chase." Mason eased out of his deceptively relaxed pose where he'd been leaning against the mashed-up fender of his pickup. "Your visitors have arrived."

Marty had straightened from studying her artwork for the hood, no longer casually leaning on the fender, but standing stiff and controlled. Charlie clutched Zoe a little tighter as Chase came to stand beside her and the Calhouns closed rank around her.

"I can see that." He dropped the manila folder on the hood of Mason's pickup. "I knew I should have taken the shotgun from the safe this morning."

"I heard there's a party going on." Carter breezed into the garage. "I was in town for some supplies and thought I'd join in. Thanks for the heads-up, Mase. I brought the shotgun and a shovel. In case, you know … we need to hide the bodies. There's a saying out here that everyone dies famous in a small town. It's true."

"Clearly something this family is familiar with. What's that? Two murders in twenty-five years? Charlotte." Tony eased out of his stare down with Marty to cast a glance at his daughter. "The car's outside. Get in it."

Chase captured Charlie's hand in his and held it tight.

"Charlie doesn't respond to commands."

"I thought I'd made it clear to *Charlotte* what would happen if she didn't respond." Tony's gaze dropped to their joined hands. "But I can see that she has manipulated her way into your trust. And like everything my daughter touches, it will be your downfall."

"You're actually related to these assholes, Pyro?" Mason tested the weight of the wrench in his hand, flexing and rotating his wrist. "I'd never have guessed. You must have been raised by the housekeeper. You have far better manners."

"A lot prettier too." Carter held up a hand at Ronan's glare. "Just sayin'."

Marty leaned against the hood of Mason's pickup and tried to hide his shaking hands by folding his arms. A shake that didn't come from fear but could be interpreted as a weakness rather than the illness it resulted from. Chase hated that his father, who'd always been strong, was being made weak by his misbehaving nervous system. If it wasn't for his Parkinson's, he'd march the Jacksons right back out the door and throw them out on the street himself.

"Still relying on Sullivan to do your dirty work, Tony? No different from the old days, right? Dig up the dirt, dish it out, and wallow in the spoils when the mud's thrown." Marty shook his head, the uncontrolled tic only barely visible in the movement. "Thought you'd be man enough to fight your own battles, win your own races, now that you've grown up."

"And I heard you're finished, Calhoun. So, bringing you down further should be easy. Must be hard for a man like you to fall so far."

Charlie tore her hand from Chase's grasp and stepped forward, her voice shaking. "Stop it. Your fight isn't with the Calhouns. It's with me."

"Everything with you is a confrontation, Charlotte. It doesn't need to be. Hand over the baby, and I'll make sure you have enough money to live comfortably wherever you please."

"Do you really think your five million dollars will stretch that far? I've told you before, my baby's not for sale."

"I can have the baby taken or you can hand her over, but this is a done deal. I won't be leaving without her. You said you wanted to come to an agreement. You hand over the child, I take her, you go away quietly. We have an agreement."

Cold seeped through her. Zoe, wide awake and alert to the tension, clutched at her sweater. "You really think it's that easy, don't you? She's just a commodity, something you can trade. Do you know what the Diegos plan to do with her?"

"What happens once we hand her over is not my concern. Or yours. That's the point of adoption."

"Except this isn't adoption, is it? This is knowingly selling a child into a corrupt world. You're committing a crime." Her heart ached that he couldn't see past the transaction to the lives he was destroying.

"You have no proof that there is money involved."

Chase threaded his fingers through hers, his touch firm and reassuring. "An investigation into your bank accounts will tell a different story. Besides the fact that you've just tried to bribe Charlie, this isn't about money, Jackson. It's about your daughter. And your granddaughter."

"You have no idea what this is about. Get in the car, Charlotte. I'm done talking to these backwater yahoos." He shoved Ronan toward the door. "This is my business and if you insist on interfering, Sullivan will leak a story to the press on how you killed your mother. And then your sister better watch her back on that track."

"No one is going to believe that a ten-year-old boy murdered his pregnant mother. Not when all the testimonies and evidence can prove it wasn't anything more than an accident. I dare you to make it more than that. You'll lose. It would all be lies, and you know it, Tony." Chase's voice was calm with a no-more-bull undertone. "And lies have a habit of tripping a person up, even decades later."

Her father stiffened, his eyes narrowing. "You think you've got something on me, Calhoun? You're mistaken."

"You can always test the theory and find out, but I have evidence of another deal that went on … under the sheets … back in ninety-two. It would be a shame if the rumors resurfaced and the racing council got wind of it. People will look at you in a completely different light and your son's career will be over. Where have you got more to lose?" Chase stared her father down.

"I have no idea what you're talking about. You're stalling. Wasting my time."

Marty stepped in and picked up the manila folder. "He's got a lot more to lose, haven't you, Tony? This file proves that the race officials have been known to turn a blind eye. The same way your mother did, Charlie."

Charlie frowned. "My mother?"

Marty nodded. "I know things from my track days that would make great gossip rag stories, but that information should be used for good not evil. It took some talking and reminiscing, but eventually your mother agreed to let me release the independent report on that final race. She's been living in her own kind of jail, Charlie."

"It was in a very extravagant cell then." Charlie couldn't stop the bitterness from coloring her tone.

"Sometimes we have to make hell look pretty, honey." Marty dropped the folder on the hood of the pickup. "It's time to lay these ghosts to rest." He took a breath and let it out on a sigh, hiding the shake of his hands by shoving them into his pockets. "Way back in ninety-two before Nora's accident brought me home, there was a bit of a scandal on the track. Tony won a race he shouldn't have. That night at the after-party, I stumbled in on something I wasn't meant to see. Let's just say that one of the race officials was more than just a friend. Your father has been living his own lie, Charlie. His marriage to your mother was a complete sham. He's always wanted to be with someone else, but he needed a cover-up that wouldn't sully the Jackson family name and strip him of his trust account, so he married your mother."

"That's a lie, Calhoun." The lack of conviction in his words told a different story.

They had him on the back foot. Charlie held Chase's hand a little tighter. "Is it, Dad? It would explain so much. The long absences, the separate rooms, the lack of affection." She held her father's gaze. "An ongoing affair that, if leaked to the press, would be highly publicized and expose a revered member of the association? That's not the kind of information you want made public."

Tony looked away. "That's blackmail, Charlotte."

"It's no different to what you've threatened the Calhouns with. What you're planning to do with Zoe is a lot worse, Dad."

"I can't back out of this deal."

"It's not a deal, it's a crime," she reminded him.

"It would end TRJ Racing."

"You were quite happy to ruin Charlie's reputation, not to mention sell your granddaughter into a very black market," Chase threw back. "It's not your son's career you're worried about or your daughter's welfare; it's the great Jackson name. You're living your dream through your son, Tony." He took the folder from Marty. "By all accounts in this report, you never were a very good driver." He turned to Ronan. "You want to know why you father drives you so hard? It's because he couldn't make the cut himself without cheating or bribing the race officials. And that's why he wants to sell Charlie's baby. So, he can buy you a race win.

Like he had to buy his own."

Ronan stood silent, all attitude knocked from him, the shock on his face proof he hadn't known how far his father would go, that he'd had no idea where the money was to come from to continue to fund his career. What lies had her father told him too?

"Well, if the boy was competent enough to drive, I wouldn't have to do put my ass on the line for him. All those hours of training, coaching, driving ... all for *nothing*. As useless as his damn sister to me. Can't drive for shit. I gave him everything he ever wanted to encourage him, and all he did was let me down."

Charlie's words whispered softly into the sudden silence. "It doesn't feel so good to be on the receiving end, does it, Ronan? How does it feel to know that all you are is a means to an end?"

Ronan stared at his father, disbelief stealing the anger from him. "You busted my balls. Not because you believed in me, but because you wanted to make yourself look good?"

"Do you think I'm investing five million dollars in you for the hell of it?"

"Money he'll get from selling my child to his sponsor. Did you even think about where the money was coming from, Ronan?" Charlie let go of Chase's hand to unwrap a tearful Zoe. "Meet your niece. Her name is Zoe. She's three months old. This is who your father is selling to fund your win. She's become a commodity he'll trade for the good of the Jackson name. Look at her and tell me if you think that's fair." She held Zoe close as she showed her to her brother. "I've always taken the back seat to make way for you, Ronan. I've been bullied and punished so you can have what Dad wants for you. I've put up with you being mean to me in public, ridiculing me in front of your friends, and arrested and humiliated for your entertainment. I'm sorry I set fire to your car, but damn it, enough is enough."

Ronan looked at Zoe's face and avoided Charlie's completely. The sneer hadn't yet left his voice as reality punched a hole in everything he'd built his dreams on. "Since it seems to be the day for confessions, the car wasn't your fault, Charlotte. I paid Ricky to set you up. I hated you for the freedom you had while I was busting my ass on the track. The more you rebelled, the happier it made me because I thought the focus would shift to you eventually. But that's not what happened at all. The more Dad ignored you, the more attention he paid me. And that wasn't always fun and party games."

"Shut your mouth, boy," Tony roared, surging forward and startling a cry from Zoe.

Ronan took a step toward him and shoved him back. "No, Dad. I'm done keeping quiet. Charlotte, I'm sorry for making your life hell. I'm sorry it's come to this."

Ronan reached out and touched the soft skin of Zoe's cheek, catching a tear and surprising her into breathy sobs. "There's been enough destruction in this family. I've closed my eyes to so much that's been happening, because I've been made afraid of the truth. I'm taking back my power." He turned to his father. "I quit. You can find yourself another driver. And it won't be at the expense of this family. We're done here, Dad."

"Great," Carter said. "Can I shoot him now?"

"No." Sheriff Hutchins walked into the garage. "But I've sure heard enough to launch an investigation into criminal activities. There's another saying we have out here. It goes 'the best thing about living in a small town is when you don't know what you're doing, someone else does'. Tony Jackson, I think we need to talk. Your buddy, Ed Sullivan, had a lot to tell me. Seems he's willing to whistle 'Dixie' under pressure and not afraid to drop your ass right in it." He pulled the cuffs from his belt. "Selling your daughter's baby? That's low, man."

"You set me up." Disbelief echoed in her father's voice as the sheriff prepared to read him his rights.

"You set yourself up by doing a deal with the Diegos. It didn't have to come to this. Your obsession with a win and being in control has cost you big this time. But someone like you doesn't understand the importance of family and just how great that cost is. You never will now." Charlie's throat ached with regret. Maybe one day he'd realize the harm he'd done, but she wouldn't hold her breath on him changing his ways.

Sheriff Hutchins led her father away. At the door into the showroom, he turned to Ronan. "I'll need to take a statement from you given that you came here with the intention of aiding your father in this transaction."

"I had no idea there was money involved." Ronan's protest was silenced with a warning look from the sheriff.

"You showed up with him knowing what it was about. That's enough for me. I'll give you ten minutes to make your apologies. When you're done here, come down to the station. Young Mason will bring you in. Don't even think about trying to leave town," he warned.

As the showroom door closed behind them, reaction set in, relief flooding Charlie. They'd won. Her baby was safe. She could keep Zoe. Ronan reached out to touch her, but Charlie pulled away. "Don't touch me."

He let his hand fall away. "Charlotte, I had no idea what Dad had planned. I swear I never knew about the deal. I can't believe he'd sink that low."

"The apple doesn't fall far from the tree. You've been right there with him for years. Making my life hell, making a fool of me at every chance you had." Years of bottled anger bubbled up and spilled over. "Do you think an apology will be enough? Just because you made one right choice in your life doesn't mean everything else you've done to me is erased, Ronan."

He toed the floor with his boot. "I get it, Charlotte. I didn't before, but now I do."

"Shoulda got your head out your ass a long time ago, Jackson." Chase's presence warmed her back, filling her with strength. She leaned into him and welcomed the weight of his arm around her shoulders. "You have got some big bridges to mend."

Ronan agreed. "I know, but you need to know that it hasn't been all sunshine, rainbows and lollipops for me either."

Looking down at Zoe, Charlie sighed. "I don't know anything of your life because I was never a part of it. I don't even know you, Ronan. I'm not even sure I *want* to know you." Her voice cracked on the words, her throat tight. She looked up to see regret in her brother's eyes.

"I guess I deserve that." He blew out a shaky breath. "Maybe one day when things have settled down, you'll give me a chance to make it right."

Chase squeezed her shoulder reassuringly, the warmth in them seeping through her. "It's over, Charlie. Your baby is safe and your future secure. Don't you think it's time to let go of the past?"

"I'd like to, but I can't erase years of bullying and manipulation. We have to find each other again. Find ourselves."

"Then take that chance with both hands. I know what it's like to lose a brother and a mother, and I'd give anything to have them back. You have a chance to make things right, be the bigger person. To forgive. You've grown so much in the time you've been away from them. For the better. Look how much you've done for us in the time you've been here. Mistakes have been made, Charlie, but you can't hold that against your brother when some of the choices he made were not his own."

Charlie looked up at him and soaked up the affection she

saw in his eyes. "I need time."

"Then let your brother stay awhile. Take all the time you need."

Chase's arm tightened around her and she pressed closer into his side. "What about the threat to Trinity? Can you forgive him for that? Because I'm not sure I can," she said.

"What threat?" Ronan shifted closer.

"Don't pretend you don't know, Ronan." Disbelief edged her tone.

"I don't know. What threat?"

Chase held Charlie a little tighter. "That you would force Trinity off the track if Charlie didn't obey your father."

"He said that?" Ronan paced the floor, his hands dragging through his hair. "Damn it, Charlotte, I'd never do that." He turned back to her. "You know how it works out there on the track. You're blind without the spotters telling you what's happening around you. Dad tells me the moves to make and when to make them. And, yes, some of those moves caused crashes, but I never once had reason to believe they were anything more than miscalculations. Mistakes. That's what racing is all about—skill, error, winning beyond all the odds against you. When you're so close in a pack, one wrong move is all it takes. Adrenalin takes over and someone else has to do the thinking for you. I was cleared of all fault by the race officials."

Chase shook his head. "Your father has been doing your thinking for a long time, even off the track. I think we proved here today that he has at least one of the officials tied up and more on the take. You and your sister have been puppets under his control for a long time, Ronan. It's time to cut those strings."

Ronan nodded. "I can start by going down to the station and giving my statement. Start sorting things out."

Chase pressed a kiss to Charlie's forehead. "Good idea. Now we've got some sorting out of our own to do. Will you trust Carter to take Zoe, Charlie? They'll go over and hang out at Molly's while Mason walks Ronan to the sheriff's office."

"Why Carter? Are you saying I'm not grown up enough to handle a baby? Carter's younger than me and he's the one with the gun," Mason protested.

"Yeah, that's not it, Mase. Have you seen your hands? Carter's are at least clean." Chase took the shotgun from Carter's hands, unloaded it, and placed it against the pickup. "And we're not going to need the shotgun. Not today."

Mason studied his hands, covered in grime from working on his pickup. "Right," he agreed, drawing the word out.

Charlie handed Zoe over to Carter. "You take good care of her, okay?" She reached out to hug Marty hard. "Thank you for having my back. We have a lot to learn from your family."

"You are our family now." Marty patted her hand then followed his sons out the door.

Charlie watched them leave the garage, comfortable in the knowledge her baby would be safe in the hands of her new family. She turned to Chase and found him leaning against Mason's pickup, arms folded, boots crossed at the ankles.

"It's all over," he murmured, arms folded over the Calhoun logo on his chest.

"I guess. I don't know what to think."

"There's a lot to work through. It's not going to be an easy time ahead."

She studied his face, the frown on his brow, the eyes that knew her deepest secrets and had seen her worst scars. "I have bridges to mend too. I thought my mother was simply cold and distant, disinterested in her children. More interested in her celebrity lifestyle. If only she'd told me, but she was never one for heart-to-heart talks."

"Keeping secrets would do that. She's had a lifetime of pretending to be someone she's not. Not too different from you, Charlie." He held out his hands for hers.

"I guess you can never tell what's behind the masks people wear, can you?" She stepped closer to him.

"And now it's time to throw those masks away and start afresh." He uncrossed his boots.

"I like it here. Bigfork feels like home in a way Florida never did."

"Then stay." He smiled that smile that made her heart leap.

She took another step closer, boot-to-boot with him. "Where will Zoe and I stay?"

"Where do you want to be?"

"With you. In the cabin on the ranch."

He spread his legs, held open his arms for her to step into warmth of the space he created. "I think I can work with that. But we're moving to your room. I don't want you up and down the stairs in the night, checking on Zoe. I'll add another room for her. Maybe a few more bedrooms too. Are you okay with that?"

She linked her fingers behind his head, brought her face close to his. "How many bedrooms?"

"Does six seem like a good number?" He whispered the question against her lips, making her shiver.

She pressed further into his embrace as his arms tightened around her. "I think it's a good solid number."

"I think we should get some practice in. I know a place upstairs with an old back seat out of a Dodge Charger. It's where I found a sandwich thief once."

Charlie grinned against his lips, love for him warming her through, chasing away the last shadows of doubt. "I love you, Chase Calhoun. And your crazy brothers. And your father and Molly. For the first time in my life, I feel like I truly belong, that I finally have a real family."

"A custom-designed family." He kissed her long and slow, heat simmering between them with all the time in the world to ignite to a flame. She sank into the taste and feel of him, his hands and the magic they weaved on her skin. "How long do you think they'll give us alone?" he asked, coming up for air.

"I hope at least a little while, because I've got a lot to thank you for right now. But I've got a lifetime for that." She let her hands trace the contours of his face, a view she would wake up to every morning for a lifetime.

His hands cupped her hips, traced her curves until he

reached the zipper on her denims. He pressed his face into her throat and trailed kisses along her skin. "I love you, Charlotte Jackson."

"Charlie. Charlotte ran away and grew up. Charlie is here to stay."

"Charlie Jackson, will you stay with me forever and steal my chicken salad sandwiches for the rest of our lives? In return, I will love you for who you truly are and be the best dad to Zoe I could possibly be."

"How can I refuse an offer like that? Charlie Calhoun—custom designer, wife, partner, future mother to another generation of Calhouns. It has a nice ring to it."

She kissed him until the last of her fears faded, happy he held her tight because her knees had turned liquid. She didn't object when he swept her up in his arms and carried her to the back of the garage, or when he made her walk up the stairs to the attic, staying close behind her in case she took a misstep.

And when they reached the seat of the Charger with the blanket still thrown across it, he whispered, "The ghosts are gone, Charlie. I'm no longer afraid of the attic. And it's all because I found you here."

Love filled her heart. "I'm glad." And when she kissed him to make him forget any fears that remained, she could have sworn she heard his mother's sigh, before it faded, and the only sounds left were their own whispers.

The End

The Calhouns of Montana Series

Book 1: *Montana Baby*

Book 2: *Montana Daughter*

Book 3: *Montana Son*

Available now at your favorite online retailer!

About the Author

Juanita graduated from the Australian College QED, Bondi with a diploma in Proofreading, Editing and Publishing, and achieved her dream of becoming a published author in 2012 with the release of her debut romantic suspense, *Fly Away Peta* (recently re-released as *Under Shadow of Doubt*).

Under the Hood followed in 2013 as one of the first releases from Harlequin's digital pioneer, Escape Publishing.

In 2014 Juanita was nominated for the Lynn Wilding (Romance Writers of Australia) Volunteer Award, and was a finalist in the Romance Writers Australia Romantic Book of the Year and the Australian Romance Readers Awards in

2014 and 2016. Her small-town romances have made the Amazon bestseller and top 100 lists. Juanita writes mostly contemporary and rural romantic suspense but also likes to dabble in the ponds of Paranormal with Greek gods brought to life in the 21st century.

She escapes the real world to write stories starring spirited heroines who give the hero a run for his money before giving in. When she's not writing, Juanita is mother to three boys and a Daschund named Sam, and has a passion for fast cars and country living.

Author Site: juanitakees.com
Facebook: facebook.com/juanitakeesauthor
Twitter: @juanitakees

Thank you for reading

Montana Baby

If you enjoyed this book, you can find more from all our great authors at TulePublishing.com, or from your favorite online retailer.

TULE
PUBLISHING

CPSIA information can be obtained
at www.ICGtesting.com
Printed in the USA
LVHW052335070921
697192LV00008B/956

9 781951 786694